# FLAUBERT

## DICTIONARY OF
## ACCEPTED IDEAS

# FLAUBERT

## DICTIONARY OF
## ACCEPTED IDEAS

*Translated, with an introduction and notes by*
**JACQUES BARZUN**

A NEW DIRECTIONS BOOK

## BIBLIOGRAPHICAL NOTE

When New Directions decided to publish an English version of *Bouvard et Pécuchet* in 1954, Mr. James Laughlin asked me to complete the translation of the *Dictionnaire des Idées Reçues*, which he knew I had been toying with for some years. I did so, and the translation appeared both with the novel and separately for the first time in the United States.

After its appearance I kept revising my text, in hopes of a second edition. That opportunity came when Max Reinhardt of London brought out under the same title a much improved text. I was still unsatisfied and kept fiddling (as well as correcting mistakes of interpretation in the notes), so as to be ready for a third chance, meanwhile circulating a longish errata list privately among friends.

A renewed demand for the little work made itself known to New Directions about 1966 and plans made for another edition, entirely reset. I pulled out my interlined copy once more and made further changes, which Mr. Laughlin gave me yet one more opportunity to add to in proofs. I am sorry to let my author go, but I think I have done all I could. There, in the words of Byron, let him *lay*.

J.B.

*December 22, 1967*

# INTRODUCTION

### by Jacques Barzun

FOR SOME SIXTY YEARS NOW, French readers of Flaubert's last novel, *Bouvard and Pécuchet*, have been entertained by browsing through its supplement, the *Dictionnaire des Idées Reçues*, to which is sometimes added the *Catalogue des Idées Chic*. Half a dozen editions of this appended matter have come out in France, and for the first time as a separate work in 1951.[1] The Dictionary is of course known by reputation in England and America, better known perhaps than *Bouvard* itself; but despite some fragments rather carelessly translated in the magazine *Gentry* (Summer 1952), the little work cannot be said to have entered our literature as have Flaubert's letters and novels.

It is not surprising, therefore, that the character of the Dictionary is frequently misunderstood, for it cannot be guessed at from mere description or random quotation. Indeed, the use and effect of the substance he has left us were probably not entirely clear to Flaubert himself. The Dictionary and the dialogue of *Bouvard* show many parallels, and Flaubert may have intended that after his two disappointed heroes have given up active endeavors and started "copying" again they should in

---

[1] Jean Aubier, Editeur, 2 rue des Beaux-Arts, Paris. A further group of notes and quotations was published in 1966 by Geneviève Bollème under the title *Le second volume de Bouvard et Pécuchet* (Paris, Les Lettres Nouvelles). The new matter does not add to the force of the demonstration, being second-hand rather than original.

fact collect and copy the materials of the Dictionary, together with the quotations of the so-called Album or anthology of absurdities. Both works exhibit specimens of the same conventional stupidity. But the alphabetful of definitions we have here is compiled from a mass of notes, duplicates and variants that were never even sorted, much less proportioned and polished by the author. We therefore do him an injustice in calling these flying sheets a "work". More than one of them would very likely have been discarded as his intention grew clearer in the task of revision.

What is perfectly clear is Flaubert's attitude towards the objects of his satire. We know his state of mind from *Bouvard*, from the letters, from innumerable anecdotes. Travelling by train during the time he was composing the novel, he was accosted by a stranger: "Don't you come from So-and-so and aren't you a traveller in oil?" "No," said Flaubert, "in vinegar." From infancy, we are told, he refused to suffer fools gladly; he would note down the inanities uttered by an old lady who used to visit his parents, and by his twentieth year he already had in mind making a dictionary of such remarks. And of course, like nearly every French artist since the Romantic period, he loathed the bourgeois, whom he once for all defined as "a being whose mode of feeling is low". From the early 1850's, Flaubert kept writing and talking to his friends about this handbook, this Dictionary, as his beloved work, his great contribution to moral realism. The project was for him charged with a personal emotion, not simply an intellectual one: "To dissect," he wrote to George Sand, "is a form of revenge."

Before its adaptation to the requirements of *Bouvard*, the separate Dictionary was to mystify as well as goad the ox: "Such a book, with a good preface in which the motive would be stated to be the desire to bring the nation back to Tradition, Order and Sound Conventions—all this so phrased that the reader would not know whether or not his leg was being pulled —such a book would certainly be unusual, even likely to succeed, because it would be entirely up to the minute" (to Bouilhet, 4th September 1850). The same animus against the philistine public, which hardly lets up for an instant throughout Flaubert's letters, was to find overt expression in the Dictionary, and with impunity: "No law could attack me, though I should attack everything. It would be the justification of Whatever is is right. I should sacrifice the great men to all the nitwits, the martyrs to all the executioners, and do it in a style carried to the wildest pitch—fireworks . . . After reading the book, one would be afraid to talk, for fear of using one of the phrases in it" (to Louise Colet, 17th December 1852).

All this may be called Theme 1 of the Dictionary: the castigation of the cliché. This purpose was not new with Flaubert, though it arose in him from native impulse. The captions of Daumier's drawings, the sayings of M. Joseph Prudhomme in Henri Monnier's fictional *Memoirs* of that character (1857), as well as a number of other less enduring works, testify to the nineteenth century's growing awareness of mass production in word and thought. In the one year 1879, two contemporaries of Flaubert's, the celebrated horn player and wit Eugène Vivier and the obscure L'Epine, both published brochures having the same tendency as the projected Dictionary. Flaubert read them at once and was relieved: "Nothing to fear—asinine." In spite of this summary dismissal, Vivier's *Un peu de ce qui se dit tous les jours* was quite superior to L'Epine's *Parfait Causeur* and it certainly anticipated the tone of the Flaubertian cliché: "They quarrel all day long, but really adore each other."—"With me, it's just the opposite: if I didn't drink any, I wouldn't sleep all night."[1]

The cliché, as its name indicates, is the metal plate that clicks and reproduces the same image mechanically without end. This is what distinguishes it from an idiom or a proverb. *The Dictionary of Clichés* published some years ago by Mr. Eric Partridge straddles several species of set phrases and hence bears no likeness to Flaubert's: it makes no point. The true nature of the thing Flaubert was out to capture and alphabetize was first discussed by an American in our century and endowed by him with a new name which has passed into the language: Gelett Burgess's "Are you a Bromide?" appeared as a magazine article in 1906. In book form it lists forty-eight genuine clichés (including the archetypal: "It isn't the money, it's the principle of the thing") and it makes the fundamental point that "it is not merely because this remark is trite that it is bromidic; it is because with the Bromide the remark is *inevitable*."

In reading Flaubert's Dictionary, this principle has to be borne in mind, for some of the utterances pilloried are manifestly true; they have to be said at certain times, being in themselves neither fatuous nor tautological. What damns them is the fact that they are the only thing ever said on the subject by the middling sensual man. As in the works of our modern lexicographer—Mr. Frank Sullivan's Arbuthnot, the cliché expert—the form, imagery and intention of the remarks are immediately recognized as approved, accepted, inescapable, *reçues* before they begin. In Flaubert's entourage these expressions recurred, more frequent and regular than the tides, and drove him frantic. For we should remember that he passed

[1] Vivier, *op. cit.*, pp. 3 and 99.

4

much of his life at Croisset, on the right bank of the Seine below Rouen, and was forced to listen there to much conversation that was not simply bourgeois and philistine, but invincibly repetitious and provincial. Traces of this aggravation are abundant in the Dictionary (e.g. COFFEE, COTTON, CLOTH), and one may surmise that in the finished work these local allusions would have been either eliminated or signalized as home variants of cosmic bromidism.

At any rate, to Flaubert these repetitions proved more than signs of dullness, they were philosophic clues from which he inferred the transformation of the human being under machine capitalism. This he took as a personal affront. Representing Mind, he fought the encroachment of matter and mechanism into the empty places that should have been minds. He kept seeking ways of rendering what he saw, and in addition to *Bouvard* and the Dictionary, he got as far as writing and circulating—no one would produce it—a sort of Expressionist play called *The Castle of Hearts*, of which the effect was to be "comic and sinister". The chief scene would show, through the glass walls of identical houses along a Paris street, identical bourgeois families eating identical meals and exchanging identical words to identical gestures. This of course is akin to the scheme of Zola's *Pot-Bouille* (*Restless House*) and many another attempt at literary Unanimism since: the device was in the air with the hum of machinery.

But while giving the nineteenth century its share in the formation of the bourgeois and bromide, one must not overlook a second influence at work in shaping Flaubert's material. The Dictionary frequently derides the specially French as against the European or world outlook; the stay-at-home timidity and love of the familiar which, although a universal trait, is reinforced in France by a tradition of complacency that dates back to Louis XIV. This is what Flaubert had in mind when he spoke of his work bringing back the nation to Tradition, Order and Sound Conventions. (See the comment upon the architectural orders and all the references to the causes of the Revolution.) The reception of *Salammbô* by the Paris critics, and particularly by Sainte-Beuve, illustrated for him the same self-centerdness.

To this one must add that the French language, despite its marvellous power of combining force and subtlety, is traditionally a language of clichés. Readymade expressions abound and are to be preferred; indeed it is not licit to break them up, it is "extravagant". The seventeenth-century aesthetician Père Bouhours has an anecdote on this point which has become famous—almost a cliché: a piece of writing having been shown to an "illustrious personage", this arbiter of taste smiled and said: "These words must be greatly astonished to find themselves together, for assuredly they had never met before."

It is but a few steps from this to Flaubert's "always preceded (or followed) by" and his other set devices. They all indicate a fixity, which on reflection is seen to go beyond forms of speech or lack of ideas or aimless parroting. Social in origin, it is lust for order through convention. Take, for example, Flaubert's great negative: "Thunder against" (*tonner contre*). The injunction succinctly represents the agreed-upon necessity to defend the family, property, religion—the famous "bases" of society— against attack. Nor is this a French trait exclusively. One thinks at once of Trollope's *Jupiter* and *Thunderer* newspapers thundering on the same subjects and of Mr. Podsnap leaning on his mantelpiece while he lectures about the British constitution to (it so happens) a Frenchman. Almost every social critic of the nineteenth century was persuaded that more light shone beyond the frontier, and Dickens and Flaubert are at one about the ubiquitous Podsnap underfoot.

The affirmative counterpart of "Thunder against" is "Very swank" (*très chic* or *bien porté*). This designates words and acts which deviate from the norm without undermining the "bases"; here is variety which will not bring on revolution. For revolution is the bugbear behind much of the thundering, and no reader of history can question the reality of the threat. In English-speaking countries one tends to imagine that the Continent was then freer in mind than England, precisely because it indulged in frequent uprisings. Flaubert's Dictionary should suffice to show that France had its Victorianism too. The connection between sexual and political conformity is well-known, and sexual matters, it is clear, occupy in Flaubert's definitions a place that would be disproportionate if it were not so unmistakably a cultural sign. Some of the items under this head sound fantastic to us, others quite up-to-date. Other entries, which are free from either sex or politics, remind us that democratic jealousy and competition were already strong and therefore repressed, therefore guilty and aggressive in the small ways we know so well—for example, giving your neighbor the benefit of your superior knowledge: "The only good X comes from Y."

To the extent that some of the remarks "date," the Dictionary is an admirable document. A good many sayings are inspired by the Franco-Prussian war which, as we know from Gobineau's searching essay on the débâcle, let loose an unprecedented amount of nonsense. In such circumstances the cliché becomes a shield against hard truth, humiliation and despair. And that is the moment seized by the satirist to avenge

7

himself, like a reborn Cassandra, by dissecting the present: "All our trouble," writes Flaubert to George Sand in the wretched year 1871, "comes from our gigantic ignorance ... When shall we get over empty speculation and accepted ideas? What should be studied is believed without discussion. Instead of examining, people pontificate."

In so saying, Flaubert states Theme 2 of the Dictionary—the attack on misinformation, prejudice and incoherence as regards matters of fact. Flaubert has an infallible ear for the contradictions that everybody absent-mindedly repeats: "ABSINTHE— Violent poison: one glass and you're dead. Newspapermen drink it as they write their copy." He plumbs with equal sureness the depths of well-bred ignorance—or rather his eye takes in at a glance the shoals of common knowledge: people know only two things about Archimedes, not three. Here too, in culture, art, history, science and social thought, some things are to be thundered against, others are very swank. The bourgeois mind in this department of life is a compound of error, pedantry, misplaced scorn, fatuous levity and ignorance of its ignorance.

As before in language, so again in opinion, the French tradition works towards a conventional narrowing. French textbooks repeat the same views, offer the same extracts and, lest the student should rashly venture on a perception of his own, guide him with footnotes to the correct criticism of the text: the child reads and repeats apropos of a verse or a turn of phrase: "*métaphore hardie*," "*pléonasme vicieux*," and the like. In working at *Bouvard* Flaubert consulted—or had helpers abstract for him—over a thousand works of reference or instruction, from which he culled the enormities that enliven the pages of that novel and that were also to fill out its documentary sequel. The Dictionary appears as a vestibule between two storerooms.

But the systematic hunt for howlers became dangerous to the hunter and to his plan. It is not simply that the two clerks, whose lives were first to be chronicled as *Memoirs of Two Cockroaches*, turned into subtle and ingenious spokesmen for their creator (e.g. Chapters IV and V on literature and history) but that Flaubert himself became something of a pedant. In the Dictionary he grows schoolmarmish over common expressions that are justifiable and useful, such as that which marks the contrast between warmed air in a sheltered spot and the open air which is cooler. (See Air and also Accident, Earth, Lilac.) Elsewhere he shows off minute knowledge acquired in tracking down gross errors; he grows ungenerous (Write); and in recording the many superstitions about health and hygiene, he surely confuses old peasant notions with the more reprehensible (because "educated") prejudices that have replaced the first.

He was fully aware of his danger: "The book I am working on could have as sub-title, Encyclopaedia of Human Stupidity. The undertaking gets me down and my subject becomes part of me . . ." To this immersion we may perhaps attribute a slip he would certainly have ridiculed in another writer: "Scaffold —When upon it, manage to say a few eloquent words *before dying*." I underscore the words rather than Flaubert's carelessness, for he was ready to make fun of himself under the same rubric as the bourgeois. The comment on Fulminate (a favorite verb of his) is surely directed at himself, and we know from a note in the Catalogue that he planned to include among its blunders a sentence from *Madame Bovary*.

In collecting spoken and printed nonsense Flaubert had even more predecessors than in recording clichés. The *sottisier* is an

9

old French genre, which in our day is represented by Curnonsky's *Le Musée des Erreurs* and George Jean Nathan's *Great American Credo*, as well as *The New Yorker's* vigilant scanning of the daily press. But since Flaubert did not live to write the preface to his Dictionary, the analysis of Theme 2 is lacking. For a clue comparable to Gelett Burgess's one must go to a chapter in George Campbell's *Philosophy of Rhetoric*: "Why is it Nonsense so often escapes both reader and writer?" The answer is: we think by signs, and the connectedness they have acquired as signs makes us believe in the connection of the things they stand for. Thus in the Dictionary: "ANTICHRIST—Voltaire, Renan . . ." or "LYNX—Animal famous for its eye."

Nascent specialization in Flaubert's day obviously encouraged the sin of affirming without examining and he found brilliant ways of showing this. One is the recurrent "Meaning unknown" (*on ne sait pas ce que c'est*), with its variant: "Nobody is expected to know." The other is a device that deserves to be called *Flaubertismus*. It consists in plucking out of all possible usages the two unrelated ones that are truly common and exclusive, thus "GROUP—Suitable for a mantelpiece and in politics." (See also PROSPECTS and UNLEASH.)

But like stupidity and pedantry, specialization is catching. Stendhal had pointed out long before Flaubert that "an idiot who knows a date can disconcert the wittiest man" At times Flaubert did not quite know with whom to side, the wit or the man with a date. He seems to be, as we say in our jargon, a realist. He derides angels, wings, poetry and lakes—which looks like throwing Romanticism to the dogs. But he is full of Romanticism and will not let it be wantonly attacked by anybody but himself. By reverse sarcasm he defends dreamers, poets, ideals, great men against fools, and martyrs against realists. In the end he does not take sides but knows what he thinks. About literature, politics and religion he quotes the current cant of both parties and berates it with bad puns, double entendres and forgotten jokes. What he steadily denounces, then, is not the bourgeois as such—since the poor creature cannot please him by saying either white or black—but the bourgeois "style" in the Nietzschean sense, that is to say, lack of style. The bourgeois as an historic phenomenon and a live obnoxious neighbor is lost in a frontal assault on what has been the enemy all along—lack of passion and imagination.

Though all these are large targets and strong hatreds, their presence is conveyed for the most part by irony and innuendo and in the most laconic French imaginable. The task of the translator can thence be inferred as more than usually arduous. To give anything like the impression of the original, he must be just as natural and fully as quick. Yet he must jump the language barrier from cliché to cliché while carrying from one culture and background to their counterparts what "everybody knows"—or doesn't know. He is continually beset by dilemmas, tempted by lesser advantages, threatened by ambiguities. Whether to take the obvious but factually different equivalent; whether to make clear what the English requires if any meaning is to emerge, even though the French is content with a vagueness that is wholly intelligible; whether to say "you" for "*on*"— the pronoun which Flaubert would have had to invent had it not already existed: *on dit, on ne sait pas*; whether to render identical expressions identically throughout, at the cost of one misfit out of three; whether to omit or re-invent—these and a multitude of other questions arise at every turn, sometimes two or three abreast in one definition.

I shall not argue here for the points of method I have followed,[1] but simply list some of the compromises I have made, mentioning at the same time that the notes marked "Fr" give the significant French word wherever a wide leap of denotation was taken for the sake of indispensable immediacy of understanding. I have used quotation marks much more freely than Flaubert, to stress the thing said as against the mere belief; I have used analogies from English and American life, tags from English and American authors, just like changes in denotation, for immediacy; I have felt similarly free in mixing tones, using our century's colloquialisms side by side with such expressions as "Thunder against" and "Wax indignant," which I felt were Flaubert's just levy on his contemporaries' idiom.

Finally, I have combined certain entries under one head, for convenience, or perforce when there was but one English word for two French synonyms that Flaubert had treated separately (FEU, INCENDIE). The twenty-one items of the *Catalogue des Idées Chic* were left out as being too fragmentary and often too parochial. The notes upon it would have taken more room than the list itself, and the impression of so much semi-recondite matter would have spoiled whatever unity of effect had been achieved in rendering the Dictionary. It also, one cannot too frequently repeat, is but a mass of notes out of a folder. Would that all our scattered papers held half so insidious an appeal to later minds!

[1] Readers interested in problems of translation will find my views stated at some length in an article published in *Partisan Review* for November–December 1953.

# A

ABELARD. No need to have any notion of his philosophy, nor even to know the titles of his works. Just refer discreetly to his mutilation by Fulbert. The grave of Abelard and Heloïse: if someone tells you it is apocryphal, exclaim: "You rob me of my illusions!"

ABSALOM. If he had worn a wig, Joab could not have murdered him.[1] Facetious name for a bald friend.

ABSINTHE. Extra-violent poison: one glass and you're dead. Newspapermen drink it as they write their copy. Has killed more soldiers than the Bedouin.[2]

ACADEMY, FRENCH. Run it down, but try to belong to it if you can.

ACCIDENT. Always "regrettable" or "unlucky"—as if a mishap might sometimes be a cause for rejoicing.

ACHILLES. Add "fleet of foot": people will think you've read Homer.

ACTRESSES. The ruin of young men of good family. Are fearfully lascivious; engage in "nameless orgies"; run through fortunes; end in the poorhouse. "I beg to differ, sir: some are excellent mothers!"

~~~~~~~~~~~~~~~~~~~~~~~~~~~~~~~~~~~~~~~~~~~~~~~~~~~~~~~~

[1] Allusion to Samuel II, 18.
[2] Allusion to the French conquest of Algeria.

ADMIRAL. Always brave. Invariable swear-word: "Shiver my timbers!"[1]

ADVERTISING. Large fortunes are made by it.

AFFAIRS (BUSINESS). Come first. A woman must not refer to hers. The most important thing in life. Be-all and end-all.

AGRICULTURE. One of the two nourishing breasts of the state (the state is masculine, but never mind). Should be encouraged. Short of hands.

AIR. Beware of drafts of air. The depths of the air are invariably unlike the surface. If the former are warm, the latter is cold, and vice versa.

ALABASTER. Its use is to describe the most beautiful parts of a woman's body.

ALBION. Always preceded by white,[2] perfidious or Positivist. Napoleon only failed by a hair's breadth to conquer it. Praise it: "freedom-loving England."

ALCIBIADES. Famous for his dog's tail. Typical debauchee. Consorted with Aspasia.

ALCOHOLISM. Cause of all modern diseases. (See ABSINTHE and TOBACCO.)

AMBITION. Always preceded by "mad," unless it be "noble."

AMERICA. Famous examples of injustice: Columbus discovered it and it is named after Amerigo Vespucci. If it weren't for the discovery of America, we should not be suffering from syphilis and phylloxera.[3] Exalt it all the same, expecially if

---

[1] Fr: "Mille sabords!"
[2] Because of the white cliffs of Dover.
[3] Disease of the grape. In point of fact, when phylloxera nearly killed off the French vines in 1896, they were restored by grafting American plants.

you've never been there. Lecture people on self-government.

AMPHITHEATER. You will know of only one, that of the Beaux-Arts School.

ANDROCLES. Mention him and his lion when someone speaks of animal tamers.

ANGEL. Eminently suitable for love and literature.

ANGER. Stirs the blood: healthful to yield to it now and then.

ANIMALS. "If only dumb animals could speak! So often more intelligent than men."

ANT. Model to cite in front of a spendthrift. Suggested the idea of savings banks.

ANTICHRIST. Voltaire, Renan . . .

ANTIQUES. Always modern fakes.

ANTIQUITY (AND EVERYTHING CONNECTED WITH IT). Out of date, an awful bore.

APARTMENT (BACHELOR'S). Always in a mess, with feminine garments strewn about. Stale cigarette smoke. A search would reveal amazing things.

APLOMB. Always "perfect" or "diabolical."

APRICOTS. "None to be had again this year."

ARCHIMEDES. On hearing his name, shout "Eureka!" Or else: "Give me a fulcrum and I will move the world" There is also Archimedes' screw, but you are not expected to know what it is.

ARCHITECTS. All idiots: they always forget to put in the stairs.

ARCHITECTURE. There are but four architectural orders. Forgetting, of course, the Egyptian, Cyclopean, Assyrian, Hindoo, Chinese, Gothic, Romanesque, etc.

15

ARISTOCRACY. Despise and envy it.

ARMY. The bulwark of society.

ARSENIC. Found in everything. Bring up Mme. Lafarge.[1] And yet certain peoples eat it.

ART. Shortest path to the poorhouse. What use is it since machinery can make things better and quicker?

ARTISTS. All charlatans. Praise their disinterestedness (*old-fashioned*). Express surprise that they dress like everyone else (*old-fashioned*). They earn huge sums and squander them. Often asked to dine out. Woman artist necessarily a whore. What artists do cannot be called work.

ASP. Animal known through Cleopatra's basket of figs.

ASSASSIN. Always a coward, even when he acted with daring and courage. Yet less reprehensible than a firebug.

ASTRONOMY. Delightful science. Of use only to sailors. In speaking of it, make fun of astrology.

ATHEISTS. "A nation of atheists cannot survive."

AUTHORS. One should "know a few," never mind their names.

---

[1] Marie-Fortunée Lafarge (1816–1852), principal in a famous murder case (1840), in which the detection of arsenic led to a miscarriage of justice.

# B

B.A. DEGREE. Thunder against.[1]

BACHELORS. All self-centered, all rakes. Should be taxed. Headed for a lonely old age.

BACK. A slap on the back can start tuberculosis.

BAGNOLET.[2] Town that is famous for its blind people.

BALDNESS. Always "premature," caused by youthful excesses— or by the hatching of great thoughts.

BALLOONS. Thanks to them, man will one day reach the moon. "But it will be many a day before you can steer them."

BALLS. Use this word only as a swear word, and possibly not even then. (See DOCTOR).

BANDITS. Always "fierce."

BANKERS. All millionaires. Levantines. Wolves.

BARBER. "To go to the tonsorial artist"; "to patronize Figaro." Louis XI's barber.[3] Formerly surgeons, used to bleed you.

BASES (OF SOCIETY). I.e. property, the family, religion, respect for authority. Show anger if these are impugned.

BASILICA. Grandiose synonym for church. Always: "an impressive basilica."

---

[1] Because of the competitive oral examination, thought to be haphazard and unfair.
[2] Small town near Paris where one of the earliest homes for the blind was established.
[3] Olivier le Daim, who became a favored adviser of the king's. After his master's death he became so ostentatious with his riches that he was imprisoned and hanged.

BASQUES. The people who turn out the best runners.

BATTLE. Always "bloody." There are always two sets of victors: those who won and those who lost.

BAYADÈRE. Word that stirs the fancy. All oriental women are bayadères. (See ODALISQUES.)

BEAR. Generally named Bruin.[1] Tell the story of the invalid who, seeing that a watch had fallen into the bear pit, went down and was eaten alive.

BEARD. Sign of strength. Grown too thick, will cause baldness. Helps protect neckcloth.

BEDROOM. In an old chateau, Henry IV always spent one night there.

BEER. Do not drink beer if you wish to avoid colds.

BEETHOVEN. Do not pronounce Beathoven. Be sure to gush when one of his works is being played.

BELLOWS. Never use them.

BELLY. Say "abdomen" in the presence of ladies.

BIBLE. The oldest book in the world.

BILL. Always too large.

BILLIARDS. A noble game. Indispensable in the country.

BIRD. Aspire to become one, saying with a sigh: "Oh, for a pair of wings! Wings!"—it shows a poetic soul.

BLACK AS. Follow invariably with "your hat" or "pitch". As for "jet black," what is jet?[2]

---

[1] Fr: "*Martin*."
[2] The original points out a confusion between homonyms: *geai*, a bluebird, mistakenly thought to be a black bird, and *jais*, jet.

BLONDES. Hotter than brunettes. (See BRUNETTES.)

BLOOD-LETTING. Have yourself bled in the Spring.

BLUESTOCKING. Term of contempt applied to women with intellectual interests. Quote Molière in support: "When the compass of her mind she stretches . . ."[1]

BOARDING SCHOOL. Say this in English when it is for girls.

BODY. If we knew how our body is made, we wouldn't dare move.

BOILED DINNER. Healthful. Inseparable from "broth and—."[2]

BOILS. See PIMPLES.

BOOK. Always too long, regardless of subject.

BOOTS. In summer heat, never omit allusions to policemen's boots or postmen's shoes (permissible only in the country, in the open). Boots are the only elegant footgear.

BREAD. No one knows what filth goes into it.

BREASTWORKS. Never use to refer to a woman.[3]

BREATH. To have a strong breath is a sign of distinction. Fend off remarks about killing flies. Refer it to the stomach.

BRETONS. All good souls, but stubborn.

BRONZE. Metal of the classic centuries.

BRUNETTES. Hotter than blondes. (See BLONDES.)

---

[1] "When the compass of her mind she stretches
    To tell a waistcoat from a pair of breeches."
This is the upper limit assigned to woman's intellect by Chrysale in *Les Femmes Savantes*, Act. II, Sc. VII.
[2] Fr: *"La soupe et le bouilli,"* i.e. boiled beef and the soup made from the water in which the meat was cooked.
[3] Fr: *"garde côte,"* a pun on "coast guard" and "rib protector."

BUDDHISM. "False religion of India." (Definition in Bouillet's Dictionary, first edition.)[1]

BUDGET. Never balanced.

BUFFON. Put on lace cuffs before writing.

BULL. Father of the calf; the ox is only the uncle.

BUREAUCRAT. Inspires awe, no matter what bureau he works in.

BURIAL. Too often premature. Tell stories of corpses that had eaten an arm off from hunger.

BUTCHERS. Appalling in times of revolution.

BUYING AND SELLING. The goal of life.

---

[1] Marie-Nicolas Bouillet was a prolific compiler of handbooks. His *Dictionnaire classique de l'antiquité sacrée et profane* first appeared in two volumes in 1826 and was re-issued dozens of times.

# C

CABINET MAKER.[1] Craftsman who works mostly in mahogany.

CAMARILLA. Wax indignant on hearing this word.[2]

CAMEL. Has two humps and the dromedary one; or the camel has one and the dromedary two—it *is* confusing.

CANDOR. Always "disarming". One is either full of it or wholly without.

CANNONADE. Affects the weather.

CANNONBALL. The air current it creates causes blindness.

CAP (SKULL). Indispensable to the man of letters. Gives dignity to the face.

CARBUNCLE. See PIMPLES.

CARRIAGE. It's better to rent than to own one—you're spared the bother about grooms and horses, who are always getting sick.

CARTHUSIANS. Spend their time making chartreuse, digging their own graves and saying to one another, "Brother, thou too must die."

CASTLE. Has invariably withstood a great siege under Philip Augustus.

---

[1] Fr: "*ébéniste*", i.e. worker in ebony.
[2] Political cant word suggesting a lobby, a caucus, a kitchen cabinet with sinister intentions.

CATHOLICISM. Has had a good influence on art.

CATS. Are treacherous. Call them "the tiger in the house." Cut off their tails to prevent vertigo.[1]

CATSPAW. Grave insult, but in the grand style, to fling at a political opponent: "Sir, you are but a catspaw of the Presidential clique." Used only from the rostrum of the Chamber.

CAVALRY. Nobler than the infantry.

CAVERNS. Usual residence of robbers. Always full of snakes.

CEDAR (OF LEBANON). The huge one at the Botanical Garden was brought over in a man's hat.

CELEBRITIES. Concern yourself about the least details of their private lives, so that you can run them down.

CELL. Always horrible. The straw is always damp. None has ever been found attractive.

CENSORSHIP. "Say what you will, it's a good thing."

CERUMEN. Human wax.[2] Should not be removed: it keeps insects from entering the ear.

CHAMBERMAIDS. Prettier than their mistresses. Know all their secrets and betray them. Always undone by the son of the house.

CHAMPAGNE. The sign of a ceremonial dinner. Pretend to despise it, saying: "It's really not a wine." Arouses the enthusiasm of petty folk. Russia drinks more of it than France. Has been the medium for spreading French ideas throughout Europe. During the Regency[3] people did

---

[1] An old superstition connected with witchcraft.
[2] Fr pun: "*cerumen*"—"*cire humaine*".
[3] Between the death of Louis XIV and the accession of Louis XV (1715–1723).

nothing but drink champagne. But technically one doesn't drink it, one "samples" it.[1]

CHATEAUBRIAND. Best known for the cut of meat that bears his name.

CHEATING (THE CUSTOMS). Is not dishonest; rather a proof of cleverness and political independence.

CHEESE. Quote Brillat-Savarin's maxim: "Dessert without cheese is like a beauty with only one eye."

CHESS. Symbol of military tactics. All great generals good at chess. Too serious as a game, too pointless as a science.

CHESTNUT. Female of the horse-chestnut.

CHIAROSCURO. Meaning unknown.

CHILBLAINS. Sign of health. Come from having warmed oneself after being cold.

CHILDREN. Give signs of a passionate attachment to all children when others are looking on.

CHIMNEY. Always smokes. Center of discussion about heating systems.

CHIMNEY SWEEP. "Winter's black swallow."

CHOLERA. You catch it from eating melons. The cure is lots of tea with rum in it.

CHRISTIANITY. Freed the slaves.

CHRISTMAS. Wouldn't be Christmas without the pudding.

CIDER. Spoils the teeth.

CIGARS. Those sold under government monopoly always "a foul smoke"; the only good ones are smuggled in.

---

[1] Fr: "*sabler*," literally "swilling," tossing off in large gulps.

CIRCUS TRAINERS. Use obscene practices.

CITY FATHERS. Thunder against apropos of street paving: "What can our city father be thinking of!"

CLARINET. Playing it causes blindness: all blind men play the clarinet.

CLASSICS. You are supposed to know all about them.

CLOTH. All from Elbeuf.[1]

CLOWN. His joints were made so in infancy.

CLUB. One should always belong to a club.[2]

CLUB (POLITICAL). Rouses ire of conservatives.[3] Confusion and argument about the right pronunciation of the word.

COCK. A thin man must invariably say: "Fighting cocks are never fat!"

COFFEE. Induces wit. Good only if it comes through Havre. After a big dinner party, is taken standing up. Take it without sugar—very swank: gives the impression you've lived in the East.

COGNAC. Most harmful. Excellent for certain diseases. A good swig of cognac never hurt anybody. Taken before breakfast, kills intestinal worms.

COITUS, COPULATION. Words to avoid. Say: "They had relations . . ."

COKE. Inseparable from Littleton.[4] Nobody knows what they

---

[1] Manufacturing town near Rouen; its cloth industry dates from the time of Louis XIV.

[2] Fr:"cercle". As the next entry shows, the word "club" was then still reserved for political groups.

[3] Because of the great club of the Revolution, the Jacobins.

[4] Fr: "Bartole et Cujas," respectively of the fourteenth and sixteenth centuries, both exhaustive commentators of Roman law.

did, but say to every law student: "You must be deep in your *Coke upon Littleton.*"

COLD. Healthier than heat.

COLONIES (OUR). Register sadness in speaking of them.

COMB (THICK). Makes the hair fall out.

COMEDY. In verse, no longer suited to our times. Still, high comedy commands respect—*castigat ridendo mores.*[1]

COMETS. Make fun of our ancestors who feared them.

COMFORT. The most valuable discovery of modern times.

COMMUNION. One's first communion—the greatest day of one's life.[2]

COMPETITION. The soul of trade.

COMPOSITION.[3] At school, a good composition shows application, whereas translation shows intelligence. Out in the world, scoff at those who were good at composition.

COMPROMISE. Always recommend it, even when the alternatives are irreconcilable.

CONCERT. Respectable way to kill time.

CONCESSIONS. Never make any: they ruined Louis XVI.

CONCUPISCENCE. Priest's word for carnal desire.

CONFECTIONERS. All the inhabitants of Rouen are confectioners.

---

[1] "Corrects behavior through laughter."

[2] An important ceremony for little boys and girls; they are dressed like brides and grooms, receive congratulations and presents, and eat the Jordan almonds that are tossed at them as they come out of the church.

[3] The correlative words are *"thème"* (writing a French passage in Latin or some other language) and *"version"* (rendering a foreign passage into French). From this grew the expression *"fort-en-thème"* to designate the industrious.

CONFINEMENT. Avoid the word; replace by "event": "When is the event expected?"

CONGRATULATIONS. Always "hearty," "sincere," etc.

CONSERVATIVE. Politician with pot belly. "A limited, conservative mind? Certainly! Limits keep fools from falling down wells."

CONSERVATOIRE. It is imperative to subscribe to its concerts.[1]

CONSPIRATORS. They feel a compulsion to write down their names on a list.

CONSTIPATION. All literary men are constipated. This affects their politics.

CONSTITUTIONAL (RULES). Are stifling us—under them it is impossible to govern.

CONSTITUTIONAL (WALK). Always take one after dinner: aids digestion.

CONTRALTO. Meaning unknown.

CONVERSATION. Politics and religion must be kept out of it.

CONVICTS. Always look it. All clever with their hands. Our penitentiaries number many a man of genius.

COOKING. In restaurants, always bad for the system; at home, always wholesome; in the South, too much spice, or oil.

COPAIBA BALSAM. Pretend not to know what it is for.[2]

CORNS. Better than a barometer. Extremely dangerous if badly cut. Cite dreadful examples of fatal consequences.

CORSET. Prevents childbearing.

---

[1] Founded in 1828, the Conservatoire concerts have remained the most notable in Paris.

[2] It was used to treat venereal disease.

COSSACKS. Eat tallow candles.

COTTON. Especially useful for putting in one's ear. One of the bases of society in the department of Seine-Inférieure.[1]

COUNTENANCE. "A winning countenance is still the best introduction."

COUNTERFEITERS. Always work below ground.

COUNTRY. People in the country better than those in towns. Envy their lot. In the country, anything goes—sloppy clothes, practical jokes, etc.

COUNTY (FAMILIES). Speak of them only with loftiest contempt.

COUSIN. Advise the young husband to beware of the young (male) cousin.

CRAYFISH. Female of the lobster.[2] Walks backward. Always call reactionaries "crayfish."

CREOLE. Lives in a hammock.[3]

CRIMINAL. Always "vile."

CRIMSON. Nobler word than red.

CRITIC. Always "eminent." Supposed to know everything, read everything, see everything. When you dislike him, call him a Zoilus, a eunuch.

CROCODILE. Imitates the cry of a child to lure men.

CROOK. Always in high society. (See SPY.)

CROSSBOW. The ideal occasion to bring up the story of William Tell.

---

[1] This was Flaubert's *département*, Rouen being its chief city.
[2] Two entries are here combined: *"Ecrevisse"* and *"Langouste"*.
[3] Since the days of Napoleon's wife Josephine, creole in the feminine has suggested to the French nothing but dark, tropical beauty.

CRUCIFIX. Looks well above a bedstead—or the guillotine.

CRUSADES. Benefited Venetian trade.

CUCKOLD. Every woman is expected to make her husband a cuckold.

CURAÇAO. The best comes from Holland, because it is made in Curaçao, one of the Antilles.

CURLICUES (AROUND A SIGNATURE). The more complicated, the more beautiful.

CUSTOMS DUTIES. Rebel against, and try to cheat them. (See TOLLS.)

CUT-RATE. Excellent for a shop-sign; inspires confidence.

CYPRESS. Grows only in cemeteries.

CZAR. Pronounce Tsar, and from time to time, Autocrat.

# D

DAGUERREOTYPE. Will replace painting. (See PHOTOGRAPHY.)

DAMASCUS. The only place where the art of making swords is
understood. Every good blade is from Damascus.

DANCE. 'It isn't dancing any more, it's tramping about."

DANTON. "Let us dare, and dare again, and forever dare."[1]

DARWIN. The fellow who says we're sprung from monkeys.

DAYS. The master has days: for trimming the beard, for taking a
purge, etc. And so has Madame, days which she calls "critical" at certain times of the month.

DEBAUCHERY. Cause of all diseases in bachelors.

DECORATION. The Legion of Honor: make fun of it, but covet
it. When you obtain it, say it was unsolicited.

DEFEAT. Is sustained, and is so utter that no one is left to tell the
tale.

DEICIDE. Wax indignant, despite the infrequency of the crime.

DELFT. More swank than "china."[2]

---

[1] From Danton's speech of 2nd September 1792, during the first battle of the
French armies against the coalition.

[2] Fr: "*Faïence, plus chic que porcelaine.*" It may be questioned whether this is not a
slip for the exact opposite, *faïence* being pottery and *porcelaine* china, which is to say,
vitrified pottery. The point, at any rate, is that household objects imply different
degrees of swank.

**DEMOSTHENES.** Never made a speech without a pebble in his mouth.

**DENTISTS.** All untruthful. They use "steel balm." Are said to be also chiropodists. Pretend to be surgeons, just as opticians pretend to be physicists.

**DENTURE.** Third set of teeth. Take care not to swallow while asleep.

**DERBY.** Racing term: very swank.

**DESCARTES.** *Cogito ergo sum.*

**DESERT.** Produces dates.

**DESSERT.** Deplore fact that people no longer sing at dessert. Virtuous persons scorn dessert: "Pastry! Good Lord, no! I never take it."

**DEVICE.** Obscene word.

**DEVOTION.** Complain of others' lack of it. "We have far less than a dog."

**DIAMONDS.** "The time will come when man will manufacture them!" "Believe it or not, they're nothing but a piece of coal; if we came across one in the natural state, we wouldn't bother to pick it up!"

**DIANA.** Goddess of the chaste (chased).[1]

**DICTIONARY.** Say of it: "It's only for ignoramuses!" A rhyming dictionary?—For shame!

**DIDEROT.** Always followed by "d'Alembert."

**DILETTANTE.** Wealthy man who subscribes to the opera.

**DIMPLES.** Always tell a pretty girl that little loves are hiding in her dimples.

---

[1] Flaubert writes out the pun: "*Chasse-teté*"; "*Chaste-té.*"

30

DINNER. Formerly people dined at noon. Now they dine at impossible hours. The dinner of our fathers' time is our lunch, and our lunch is their dinner; but dining so late shouldn't be called dinner: it's supper.

DINNER JACKET.[1] In the provinces, the acme of ceremony and inconvenience.

DIOGENES. "I am looking for a man." "Don't stand between me and the sun."

DIPLOMA. Emblem of knowledge. Proves nothing.

DIPLOMACY. A distinguished career, but beset with difficulties and full of mystery. Suited only to aristocrats. A profession of vague import, though higher than trade. Diplomats are invariably subtle and shrewd.

DIRECTOIRE.[2] The scandals of the time: "In those days, honor had taken refuge in the army; women in Paris went about naked."

DISCHARGE. Rejoice when it leaves the affected part, and express astonishment that the human body can contain so much matter.

DISSECTION. An outrage upon the majesty of death.

DISTINCTION. Always preceded by "rare."

DIVA. All women singers must be called divas.

DIVIDERS. Perfect eyesight has them built in.

DIVORCE. "If Napoleon had not divorced Josephine, he would still be on the throne."

DJINN. The name of an oriental dance.

---

[1] A complicated play on pronunciations is omitted here. See Fr: "*Habit noir.*"
[2] The interregnum between the Terror and Bonaparte's Consulate: 1795-1799.

DOCKYARDS.[1] Appalling in times of revolution.

DOCTOR. Always preceded by "the good." Among men, in familiar conversation, "Oh! balls, doctor!"[2] Is a wizard when he enjoys your confidence, a jack-ass when you're no longer on terms. All are materialists: "You can't probe for faith with a scalpel."

DOCTRINAIRES.[3] Despise them. Why? Nobody can say.

DOCUMENT. Invariably "of the highest importance."

DOG. Specially created to save its master's life; man's best friend.

DOGE. Wedded the sea. Only one is known—Marino Faliero.

DOLMEN. Has to do with the old Gauls. Stone used for human sacrifice. Found only in Brittany. Knowledge ends there.

DOLPHIN. Carries children on its back.

DOME. Tower with an architectural shape. Express surprise that it stays up. Two can be named: the Dome of the Invalides; that of St. Peter's in Rome.

DOMESTICITY. Never fail to speak of it with respect.

DOMINOES. One plays all the better for being tight.

DORMITORIES. Always "spacious and airy." Preferable to single rooms for the morals of the pupils.

DOUBT. Worse than outright negation.

---

[1] Fr: "*Faubourgs.*"

[2] In giving this equivalent of the French *foutre*, both here and under the letter B., there is no design to take refuge in euphemism, but only to render the exact force of the expletive. The literal equivalent would be entirely out of key and therefore inexact.

[3] A political party founded about 1815 to acclimate parliamentary institutions in France. Its principles were, briefly, checks and balances and strict adherence to principle. From Royer-Collard to Guizot, it attracted quite a few distinguished minds and exercised an influence out of proportion to its numbers.

DRAWING (ART OF). "Consists of three things: line, stippling and fine stippling. There is, in addition, the masterstroke; but the masterstroke can only be given by the master" (Christophe).[1]

DREADFUL. "Perfectly dreadful"—when alluding to words of erotic import: one may commit the act, but not speak of it. "It was at the darkest of a dreadful night."[2]

DREAMS (VAGUE). Any great ideas one does not understand.

DUCKS. Always come from Rouen.

DUEL. Thunder against. No proof of courage. Great prestige of the man who has fought a duel.

DUNGEON. Gives rise to gloomy thoughts.

DUPE. Better be a knave than a dupe.

DUPUYTREN.[3] Famous for his salve and his museum.

DUTIES. Require them of others, Avoid them yourself. Others have duties towards us, not we towards them.

DWARF. Tell the story of General Tom Thumb; if by any chance you shook his hand, boast of the fact.

---

[1] Presumably a writer of text-books, not otherwise identifiable.

[2] The line is from Racine's *Athalie*, Act II, Sc. V, and is quoted because of its complete irrelevance to what precedes. Whatever its cause, Athalie's nightmare has nothing overtly erotic about it.

[3] French surgeon (1777–1835) who died a millionaire and a baron, after having revolutionized method and taught many disciples. He left a large sum to found a museum of pathological anatomy which still exists.

# E

EARLY RISER. To be one, a sign of good morals. If one goes to bed at four in the morning and rises at eight, one is lazy; but if one goes to bed at nine in the evening and gets up the next day at five, one is a hardy type.

EARTH. Refer to its four corners since it is round.

ECHO. Mention the one in the Panthéon and the one under the bridge at Neuilly.

ECLECTICISM. Thunder against as being an immoral philosophy.

EGG. Starting point for a philosophic lecture on the origin of life.

ELEPHANTS. Have remarkable memories; worship the sun.

EMBONPOINT. Sign of elegant leisure, of utter laziness. Disagree on the pronunciation of the word.[1]

EMBRACE. "Kiss" is more decent.[2] A kiss is "gently stolen"; also "bestowed"—upon the damsel's brow, the mother's cheek, the pretty woman's hand, the child's neck and the mistress's lips.

EMIGRÉS. Earned their livelihood by teaching the guitar and waiting on table.

---

[1] This disagreement applies, in the original, to a separate entry *"Envergure,"* which having no other point is here omitted.

[2] As to this pair of words, French and English have moved in opposite directions, *baiser* having come to suggest sexual intercourse while *embrasser* means simply an affectionate hug and kiss on the cheek.

EMIRE. Used only for Abd-el-Kadr.[1]

EMPIRE. "The Empire means Peace" (Napoleon III).[2]

EMPRESSES. All beautiful.

ENAMEL. The secret of this art is lost.

ENCYCLOPÉDIE. Laugh at it pityingly for being quaint and old-fashioned; even so: thunder against.

ENGINEERING. The finest career for a young man; he learns all the sciences.

ENGLISH. All millionaires.

ENGLISHWOMEN. Express surprise that they can have good-looking children.[3]

ENJOY. Obscene word.

ENTHUSIASM. Called forth exclusively by the return of Napoleon's ashes. Always "indescribable": the newspaper takes two columns to tell you so.

EPICURUS. Despise him.

EPISTOLARY (STYLE). Reserved exclusively for women.

ERA (OF REVOLUTIONS). Still going strong, since every new government begins by promising to "call a halt."

ERECTION. Said only of monuments.

EROSTRATUS.[4] Bring up in any conversation about the fires of the Commune.

---

[1] Arab leader in North Africa who resisted French colonization for fifteen years (1832–1847). He subsequently supported French rule.

[2] Quoted from the Emperor's speech at Bordeaux, shortly before the outbreak of the Crimean War.

[3] Until very recently, the stereotype of "the Englishwoman" in France depicted a mountain climber of repellent aspect, disfigured by long teeth and wearing mannish clothes.

[4] The man who gained notoriety on the day of Alexander's birth by setting fire to the temple of Diana at Ephesus. Flaubert spells his name with an H.

ESPLANADE. Only found near the Invalides.

ETRUSCAN. All antique vases are Etruscan.

ETYMOLOGY. The easiest thing in the world, with a little Latin and ingenuity.

EUNUCH. Never can have children . . . Fulminate against the castrati singers of the Sistine Chapel.

EVACUATION. Usually "copious"; always "of an alarming sort."

EVENINGS (LATE). Are decent only in the country.

EVIDENCE. Is "plain" when not "overwhelming."

EXASPERATION. Continually at its height.

EXCEPTION. Say it proves the rule, but don't venture to explain how.

EXECUTIONS (PUBLIC). Deplore the women who go to them.

EXERCISE. Prevents all diseases. Recommend it at all times.

EXPIRE. Verb applied exclusively to newspaper subscriptions.

EXTINCTION. Applies only to the national debt.[1]

EXTIRPATE. Verb applied only to heresy and corns.

---

[1] The French cliché requires "pauperism" in place of "national debt."

# F

FAÇADE (OF BUILDINGS). Great men look well when sculptured in front of.

FACE. The mirror of the soul. Hence some people's souls must be rather ugly.

FACTORY. Dangerous neighborhood.

FAITHFUL. Inseparable from "dog" and "friend." Never miss a chance to quote: "True as a needle to the pole" and "Among the faithless, faithful only he."

FAME. "Vanity of vanities."

FANFARE. Always "loud."

FAREWELL. Work a sob into your voice in speaking of Napoleon's farewell at Fontainebleau.

FARM. When visiting a farm, one must eat nothing but rye bread and drink nothing but milk. If eggs are added exclaim: "Heavens, but they're fresh! Not a chance you'd find any like these in the city!"

FARMER. Always "Squire" So-and-so. All easy-going.

FARMERS. What would we do without them?

FAT. Fat people do not need to learn to swim. Are the despair of executioners owing to the difficulty they present; e.g. la Du Barry.

FATAL. A wholly romantic word. Applied to a man, signifies one with the evil eye.

FAVOR. It is doing children a favor to slap them; animals, to beat them; servants, to fire them; criminals, to punish them.

FEAR. Gives wings.

FELICITY. Always "perfect." If your cook is named Felicity, she is perfect.

FEMALE. Use only in speaking of animals. Contrary to what obtains in the human race, the females of animals are less beautiful than the males, e.g. pheasant, rooster, lion, etc.

FENCING. Fencing masters know secret thrusts.

FEUDALISM. No need to have one single precise notion about it: thunder against.

FEVER. A sign of the strength of the blood. Caused by prunes, melons, the sun in April, etc.

FIGARO (MARRIAGE OF). Another of the causes of the Revolution!

FIGLEAF. Emblem of virility in the art of sculpture.

FINGER. God's finger is in every pie.

FINGERBOWLS. Sign of wealth in the household.

FIRE.[1] Purifies everything. On hearing the cry of "Fire!" begin by losing your head. A spectacle worth seeing.

FIRING SQUAD. Nobler than the guillotine. Delight of the man who is granted the favor of facing one.

FLAG. The sight of it makes the heart beat faster.

FLAGRANTE DELICTO. Always use the Latin phrase. Applies only to adultery.

---

[1] This combines two entries: *"Feu"* and *"Incendie."*

FLAMINGO. A bird, so called because native to Flanders.

FLATTERERS. Never miss the chance to quote: "By God, I cannot flatter"; and "Every flatterer lives off the fool who listens to him."

FLIES. *Puer abige muscas.*[1]

FLOOD VICTIMS. Always along the Loire.

FOETUS. Any anatomical specimen preserved in spirits of wine.

FOOD. In boarding schools, always "wholesome and plentiful."

FOREHEAD. Wide and bald, a sign of genius, or of self-confidence.

FOREIGN. A fad for everything foreign: a sign of a liberal mind; contempt for whatever is not French: a sign of patriotism.

FORK. Should always be of silver—it's less dangerous. Use it in the left hand, it is easier and more distinguished.

FORNARINA. She was a beautiful woman. That is all you need to know.

FORTUNE.[2] *Audaces fortuna juvat.* The rich are happy, they have money. When told of any large fortune, always put in, "Yes, but is it secure?"

FOSSIL. A proof of the Flood. A joke in good taste when alluding to a member of the Academy.

---

[1] "Boy! Shoo away those flies." From Cicero, *De oratore*, II, 60,247. The implication is: "Away with these importunate people!" "Musca" or fly is here a proper name as well.

[2] In French, *fortune* by itself means only wealth, whereas in the Latin phrase it means only chance, which favors the enterprising. In his first definition Flaubert dwells on the shift in meaning by equating the terms.

FOUNDATION. All news is without —.

FREE-LANCE (SOLDIER). More to be feared than the enemy.

FREEMASONRY. Yet another cause of the Revolution. The initiation is a fearful ordeal. Cause of dissension among married pairs. Distrusted by the clergy. What can its great secret be?

FREE TRADE. Cause of all business troubles.

FRENCH. The leading people in the world. "It means only one more Frenchman"[1] (said the Comte d'Artois). How proud one is to be French when gazing at the Colonne Vendôme.[2]

FRENCH FURY. Always pronounce *furia francese*.[3]

FRESCO PAINTING. No longer done.

FRICASSEE. Only good in the country.

FROG. Female of the toad.

FUGUE. Nobody knows what it consists in, but you must assert that it is extremely difficult and extremely dull.

FULMINATE. Nice verb.

FUNERAL. About the deceased: "To think that I had dinner with him a week ago." Called obsequies if it's a general; inhumation if it's a philosopher.

FUNNY. Should be used on all occasions: "How funny!"

---

[1] Allusion to an apocryphal speech of the restored Bourbon prince in 1814: "Nothing is changed; there is only one more Frenchman."

[2] Allusion is to the monument made of the enemy guns captured by Napoleon's armies.

[3] Allusion to the behavior of French armies in the Italian and Spanish wars of the fifteenth and sixteenth centuries.

FURS. Token of wealth.

FURNITURE. Be apprehensive—every kind of mishap can happen to yours.

FUSION. Of the two branches of the royal family: keep hoping for it.

# G

GAIETY. Always preceded by "mad."

GALANT HOMME. According to circumstances, pronounce *"galantuomo"* or "gentleman."

GALLOPHOBE. Use this term in speaking of German journalists.

GAME. Good only when high.

GAMIN. Always from Paris. Don't let your wife say: "When I feel gay, I love to act like a *gamin.*"

GAMING. Wax indignant at this fatal passion.

GARDENS (ENGLISH). More natural than French ones.

GARLIC. Kills intestinal worms and incites to amorous jousting. Henry IV's lips were rubbed with it at birth.

GARRET. At twenty, one can be very happy there.[1]

GARTERS. Always to be worn above the knee by society women; below it by women of the people. A woman must never neglect this point of dress—there are so many ill-bred men in the world.

GENERAL. Always "brave." Generally doing something other than his job, such as being an ambassador, alderman or head of the state.

GENERATION (SPONTANEOUS). A socialistic idea.

---

[1] Allusion to a popular song about the pleasures of being poor in youth.

GENIUS. No point admiring—it's a neurosis.

GENOVEFAN. Meaning unknown.[1]

GENTLEMEN. There aren't any left.

GEOMETRICIAN. "Travelling on strange seas of thought—alone . . ."

GERMANS. Always preceded by "blond," "dreamy"— but how efficient their army! A people of metaphysicians (*old-fashioned*). "It's no wonder they beat us, we weren't ready!"[2]

GIAOUR. Fierce expression of unknown meaning, though it is known to refer to the Orient.

GIBBERISH. Foreigners' way of talking. Always make fun of the foreigner who murders French.

GIFT. It isn't the value that gives it price, or rather, not the price that gives it value. The gift is nothing, it's the thought behind it.

GIRAFFE. Polite word to avoid calling a woman an old cow.

GIRONDISTS. "More sinned against than sinning."

GLOBE. Genteel way of referring to a woman's breasts: "May I be permitted to kiss those adorable globes?"

GLORIA.[3] Never without its *Consolation*.

GLOVES. Confer respectability.

GOBELINS. A tapestry of this kind is an amazing piece of work, it takes fifty years to make. On seeing it, exclaim: "It is more beautiful than a painting!" The workman does not even know what he is about.

~~~~~~~~~~~~~~~~~~~~~~~~~~~~~~~~~~~~~~~~

[1] Denotes a canon of the Church of Saint Genevieve.

[2] Two entries: "*Allemagne*" and "*Allemands.*" The allusion is to the French defeat of 1870.

[3] Allusion to the concluding stanza of every psalm used in the liturgy and at the same time to the popular name of coffee laced with brandy.

43

GOD. Voltaire himself admitted it: "If God did not exist, it would be necessary to invent him."

"GODDAM". The essence of the English language, as Beaumarchais said.[1] Snicker patronizingly.

GODFATHER. Always the actual father of the godchild.

"GOD SAVE THE KING". Pronounced, in Béranger's verses, "God save té King"; it rimes with *sauvé préservé, etc.* . . .

GOG. Always goes with Magog.

GOLDEN NUMBER, DOMINICAL LETTER, ETC. Shown on all calendars but nobody knows what they mean.

GORDIAN KNOT. Has to do with antiquity. (The way the ancients tied their neckties.)

GOSPELS. Divine, sublime, (and so forth), works.

GOTHIC. Architectural style which inspires religious feeling to a greater degree than others.

GOWN (A WOMAN'S). Disturbing to the fancy.

GRAMMAR. Teach it to children in earliest youth as something clear and easy.

GRAMMARIANS. All pedants.

GRAPESHOT. The only way to make the Parisians shut up.

GRATITUDE. Don't mention it.

GREATCOAT. Always the color of stone walls, for amorous adventures.

GREEK. Whatever one cannot understand is Greek.[2]

GRISETTES. There aren't any left. This is to be said with the discomfited air of the hunter who says there is no more game.

---

[1] Allusion to *The Marriage of Figaro*, Act III, Sc. V.
[2] Fr: "*Hébreu.*"

GROG. Not respectable.

GROTTOES WITH STALACTITES. At some time or other a big banquet or notable party was given there. What you see is like organ pipes. During the Revolution, Mass was celebrated there in secret.

GROUP. Suitable for a mantelpiece or in politics.

GUARD. The guard will die but won't surrender: seven words to stand for five letters.[1]

GUERRILLA. Does more harm to the enemy than the regular forces.

GUESTS. Hold them up as examples to your children.

GULFSTREAM. Famous Norwegian town, recently discovered.

GUNMEN.[2] Term used by fierce republicans to designate police officers.

GYMNASE (LE). Branch of the Comédie Française.[3]

---

[1] Allusion to the reply ("*Merde*") given by General Cambronne to the summons to surrender at Waterloo. The dressed-up "historical" version for text-book use is that given in the seven words.

[2] Fr: "*Sbires*", from the Italian *Sbirri*.

[3] This refers to a theater in Paris which for a time received a government subsidy, like the Comédie Française and others. See ODÉON.

# H

HABIT. Second nature. School habits are bad habits. Given the right habits one could play the violin like Paganini.

HAIDUK.[1] Confuse with eunuch.

HAIR (WAVING THE). Not suitable for men.

HAM. Always from Mainz. But watch out for trichinosis.

HAMLET (SMALL VILLAGE). A touching word in literature; effective in poetry.

HAMMOCK. Characteristic of creole women. Indispensable in a garden. Persuade yourself that it is more comfortable than a bed.

HAND.[2] To govern France, must be of iron; to have a beautiful hand means to have a fine handwriting.

HANDWRITING. A neat hand leads to the top. Undecipherable: a sign of deep science, e.g. doctors' prescriptions.

HANGMAN. Trade handed down from father to son.

HARD. Always add "as iron." There is also "hard as rock," but that is much less forceful.

HARE. Sleeps with its eyes open.

---

[1] Hungarian foot soldier.
[2] Two entries: *"Bras"* and *"Main."*

HAREM. Always compare a cock amid the hens to a sultan in his harem. Every college boy dreams of this.

HARP. Gives out celestial harmonies. In engravings, is only played next to ruins or on the edge of a torrent. Shows off the arm and hand.

HASHEESH. Do not confuse with hash, which produces no voluptuous sensations whatever.

HATS. Complain of their shape.

HAWSER. People have no idea how strong it is—stronger than iron.

HEALTH. Excess of health causes illness.

HEAT. Always "unbearable." Do not drink on hot days.

HELOTS. Cite as a warning to your son, though you would be hard put to it to show him any.

HEMORRHOIDS. Come from sitting on stoves and stone benches. St. Fiacre's evil. A sign of health—hence do not try to rid yourself of them.

HENRY III, HENRY IV. When mentioned, do not fail to say: "All the Henrys were unfortunate!"[1]

HERCULES. A type from the North.

HERMAPHRODITES. Arouse unwholesome curiosity. Try to see one.

HERNIA. Everybody has one without knowing it.

HEROD. To be "as old as Herod."[2]

---

[1] Both were assassinated like Henry of Guise. Henry II was killed in a tournament.
[2] An established cliché, perhaps owing to a confusion with Hesiod. But what Flaubert seems to record is another confusion, that of Herod's age with his antiquity.

HERRING. "The wealth of Holland."

HIATUS. Not to be tolerated.[1]

HICCUPS. To cure, place a large key in the middle of the back, or cause fright.

HIEROGLYPHICS. Language of the ancient Egyptians, invented by the priests to conceal their shameful secrets. "Just think! There are people who understand hieroglyphics! But after all, the whole thing may be a hoax . . ."

HIPPOCRATES. Always to be cited in Latin because he wrote in Greek, except in the maxim: "Hippocrates says Yes, but Galen says No."

HIPPOLYTUS. His death the most beautiful narrative subject that can be assigned in class. Everyone should know the piece by heart.[2]

HOME. Always a castle inviolate. However, the police and the judiciary can enter whenever they please. "Going back to my hearth and home; to my fireside."

HOMER. Never existed. Famous for his laughter.

HOMO. Say: "*Ecce homo!*" on the arrival of any person whom one is expecting.

HONOR. When mentioned, misquote: "But he that filches from me my good name doth make me poor indeed." One must always be concerned about one's own, and not greatly concerned about others'.

---

[1] The coming together of two vowels is forbidden in French verse and deprecated in French prose. It is a subject of reproof like the split infinitive.

[2] From Racine's *Phèdre*, Act V, Sc. VI, a particularly gory passage from "the gentle Racine."

HORN (HUNTING). Lovely effect in the woods, and at night across the water.

HORSES. If they knew their strength, they would not let themselves be led. Horsemeat: excellent subject for a pamphlet by a man seeking a reputation. Racehorse: despise it—of what use is it?

HOSPITALITY. Must always be Scottish. Quote: "In Scotland, hospitality when sought is given and never bought."

HOSPODAR. Sounds well in a remark on the Near East question.

HOSTILITIES. Hostilities are like oysters, they have to be opened. "Open hostilities" sounds as if one ought to sit down at table.

HOTELS. Are only good in Switzerland.

HUGO, VICTOR. "Made a sad mistake, really, when he entered politics."

HUMIDITY. Cause of every disease.

HUNCHBACKS. Are very witty. Much sought after by lascivious women.

HUNT. Good exercise, which one must pretend to love. Part of the royal state. The judiciary rave about it.

HUSSAR. Pronounce hoozar. Always preceded by "handsome" or "dashing". Attracts the ladies. Never fail to hum: "You who know a young hussar . . ."

HYDRA-HEADED (MONSTER). Of anarchy, socialism, and so on of all alarming systems. We must try and conquer it.

HYDROTHERAPY. Cure and cause of every known disease.

HYGIENE. Must be maintained. Prevents illness, except when it provokes it.

**Hypothecate.** Use the word in calling for the reform of the law governing mortgages: very swank.

**Hypothesis.** Often "rash," always "bold."

**Hysteria.** Confuse with nymphomania.

# I

ICE-CREAM MEN. All Neapolitans.

ICES. It is dangerous to eat them.

IDEALISM. The best of the philosophic systems.[1]

IDEALS. Perfectly useless.

IDEOLOGISTS. Every newspaperman is an ideologist.

IDIOTS. Those who differ with you.

IDOLATERS. Are cannibals too.

ILIAD. Always followed by "Odyssey."

ILLEGIBLE. A doctor's prescription should be. Likewise one's signature—it shows one is swamped with correspondence.

ILLUSIONS. Pretend to have had a great many, regret that you have lost them all.

IMAGINATION. Always "lively." Be on guard against it. When lacking in oneself, attack it in others. To write a novel, all you need is imagination.

IMMORALITY. Distinctly enunciated, this word confers prestige on the user.

IMPERIALISTS.[2] All honest, polite, peaceable, charming people.

---

[1] Flaubert seems to have distrusted Idealism and Materialism equally.
[2] I.e. supporters of the French Second Empire.

IMPIETY. Thunder against.

IMPORTS. Canker at the heart of Trade.

IMPRESARIO. Artist's word meaning Manager. Always preceded by "clever."

INAUGURATION.[1] Cause for rejoicing.

INCOMPETENCE. Always "notorious." The more incompetent one is, the more ambitious one ought to be.

INCOGNITO. The dress of princes on their travels.

INCRUSTATION. Applies only to mother-of-pearl.

INDIA-RUBBER. Made of horse's scrotum.

INDOLENCE. Product of warm climates.

INDUSTRY. See TRADE.

INFANTICIDE. Committed only by the lower classes.

INFINITESIMAL. Meaning unknown, but it has to do with homeopathy.

INKWELL. The ideal gift for a doctor.

INNATE IDEAS. Make fun of them.

INNOCENCE. Proved by unshakable calm.

INNOVATION. Always "dangerous."

INQUISITION. Its crimes have been exaggerated.

INSCRIPTION. Always "cuneiform."

INSPIRATION (POETIC). Brought on by: a sight of the sea, love, women, etc.

INSTINCT. Does duty for intelligence.

---

[1] This has no political implications but applies to all "openings."

INSTITUTE.[1] The members are all old men who wear green eye-shades.

INSTRUMENT. If used to commit a crime, always "blunt"— unless it happens to be sharp.

INSULT. Must always be washed out in blood.

INSURRECTION. "The holiest of duties" (Blanqui).[2]

INTEGRITY. Found particularly in judges.

INTERVAL. Invariably long.

INTOXICATION. Always preceded by "mad."

INTRIGUE. The gateway to everything.

INTRODUCTION. Obscene word.

INVALID. To raise his spirits, pooh-pooh his ailment and discount the story of his suffering.

INVASION. Brings tears to your eyes.[3]

INVENTORS. All die in the poorhouse. "The wrong man profits by their genius—it isn't fair."

ITALIANS. All musical. All treacherous.

ITALY. Should be seen immediately after marriage. Is very disappointing—not nearly so beautiful as people say.

IVORY. Refers only to teeth.

---

[1] Strictly, the name of the five academies together, but usually the name is reserved for any of the four that are not the Literary or French Academy. Thus "a member of the Institute" denotes a member of the Academy of Science, of Fine Arts, of Inscriptions or of Moral and Political Science.

[2] Professional revolutionist (1805–1881) who took the motto "Neither God nor master."

[3] Allusion to the Franco-Prussian War of 1870-71.

# J

JANSENISM. Meaning unknown, but any reference to it is swank.

JAPAN. Everything there is made of china.

JASPER. All vases in museums are of jasper.

JAVELIN. As good as a gun if you only know how to throw it.

JEALOUSY. Always preceded by "frenzied." Fearsome passion. Eyebrows that meet in the middle a sign of jealousy.

JESUITS. Have a hand in every revolution. Nobody has any idea how numerous they are. Do not refer to the "battle of the Jesuits."[1]

JEWELER. Always call him M. Josse.[2]

JEWS. "Sons of Israel." All Jews are spectacle vendors.

JOCKEY. Deplore the breed.

JOCKEY CLUB. Its members are all gay young dogs and very wealthy. Say simply, "The Jockey"—very swank: implies you belong.

JOHN BULL. When an Englishman's name is not known, he is called John Bull.

---

[1] A euphemism for pederasty. The conflict with the Jesuits in France since the 17th century supplies the needed ambiguity.

[2] Allusion to the character in Molière's *Amour médecin* who suggests jewelry as the cure for the ailing young girl. His name is now a symbol of self-profiting advice.

JOY. The mother of fun and games. Never mention her daughters

JUDICIARY. An excellent career if one wants to marry an heiress. All judges are pederasts. The robe inspires respect.[1]

JUJUBE. Made of an unknown substance.

JURY. Do everything you can to get off it.

JUS PRIMAE NOCTIS.[2] Disbelieve it.

JUSTICE. Never worry about it.

---

[1] Two entries: "*Magistrature*" and "*Robe*."
[2] The supposed right of the lord to spend the first night with the peasant's bride. Flaubert refers to its symbolic form, *Jambage*.

# K

KALEIDOSCOPE. Used only to describe picture exhibitions.

KEEPSAKE.[1] Ought to be found on every drawing-room table.

KNAPSACK. Case designed to hold marshal's baton.

KNIFE. To be called Catalonian when the blade is long; called dagger when used to commit a crime.

KNOUT. Word that offends the Russians.

KORAN. Book entirely about women, by Mohammed.

---

[1] Not a memento but the kind of anthology or annual miscellany common in the nineteenth century.

# L

LABORATORY. Have one on your country place.

LACONIC. Idiom no longer spoken.

LACUSTRIAN (TOWNS). Deny their existence, since it is obviously impossible to live under water.

LADIES. Always come first. "God bless them!" Never say: "Your good lady is in the drawing-room."

LADS. Never give a commencement address without referring to "you young lads" (which is tautological).

LAFAYETTE. General who is famous for his white horse.

LA FONTAINE. Maintain that you have never read his Tales.[1] Call him "the good La Fontaine," "the immortal maker of fables."

LAGOON. City on the Adriatic.

LAKE. Have a woman with you when you sail on it.

LANCET. Always carry one in your pocket, but think twice before using it.

LANDLORD. The human race is divided into two classes: landlords and tenants.

LANDSCAPES (ON CANVAS). Always so much spinach.

LANGUAGES (MODERN). Our country's ills are due to our ignorance of them.

---

[1] Salacious in subject though not in treatment.

LATE. "My late father"—then you raise your hat.

LATHE. Indispensable for rainy days in the country. Have one in the attic.

LATIN. The natural speech of man. Spoils one's style. Of use only for reading mottoes on public buildings. Watch how you quote Latin tags—they all have something risqué in them.

LAUGHTER. Always "Homeric."

LAURELS. Keep a man from sleeping.

LAVE.[1] Used only of the ceremonial Washing of the Feet.

LAW (THE). Nobody knows what it is.

LAWYERS. Too many in Parliament. Their judgment is warped. Of a lawyer who is a poor speaker, say: "Yes, but he knows his books."

LEAGUE. You can walk a league faster than three miles.[2]

LEARNED (THE). Make fun of. All it takes to be learned is a good memory and hard work.

LEARNING.[3] Despise it as the sign of a narrow mind. Let on that you have a fair share. The common people do not need it to earn their daily bread.

LEATHER. It all comes from Russia.

LEFTHANDED. Formidable fencers. Much more deft than those who use the right hand.

LENT. At bottom is only a health measure.

---

[1] Fr: "*Lavement*," which also means enema.
[2] A league being taken as three miles, this saying suggests the psychological difference between a single unit and its equivalent in parts.
[3] Two entries: "*Erudition*" and "*Instruction*."

LETHARGY. Some cases are known that lasted for years.

LIBERTINISM. Found only in big cities.

LIBERTY. "Liberty, what crimes are committed in thy name!"[1] "We enjoy all the liberty we need." "Liberty is not licence" (conservative tag).

LIBRARY. Always have one at home, particularly if you live in the country.

LIGHT. Always say: *"Fiat lux"* as you light a candle.

LIGUE (SIXTEENTH-CENTURY POLITICAL PARTY). Forerunners of liberalism in France.

LILAC. Delightful because it means summer is here.

LINEN. To be well dressed, one cannot display too much—or enough.

LION. Generous animal. Always plays with a large ball. "Well-roared, lion!" "To think that lions and tigers are just cats!"

LITERATURE. Idle pastime.

LITTRÉ. Snicker on hearing his name: "the gentleman who thinks we are descended from the apes."[2]

LOATHSOME. Must be said of any work of art that the *Figaro* will not let you admire.[3]

LOCKET. Must contain a lock of hair or a photograph.

LORD. Wealthy Englishman.

LORGNETTE. Insolent and distinguished.

---

[1] The words attributed to Madame Roland on the scaffold.

[2] The great French lexicographer was also a Positivist and proponent of evolutionary doctrine.

[3] The *Figaro*, founded in 1854, was a virulent satirical paper which took a strongly anti-intellectual, anti-artistic line in the name of "wit" and "common sense."

Louis XVI. Always: "that unfortunate monarch."

Lucky. Speaking of a lucky man: "He was born tagged."[1] You will not know what you are talking about and neither will your listener.

Lugger. "Come aboard my lugger, black-eyed maid of Athens . . ." (parlor song).

Luxury. The downfall of great states.

Lynx. Animal renowned for its eye.

[1] Fr: "*coiffé*," that is, born with a caul, which was deemed lucky.

# M

MACADAM. Has put an end to revolutions: barricades no longer possible. Nevertheless not so convenient as before.

MACARONI. When prepared in the Italian style, is served with the fingers.

MACHIAVELLI. Though you have not read him, consider him a scoundrel.

MACHIAVELLIAN. Word only to be spoken with a shudder.

MACKINTOSH. Scottish philosopher; invented the raincoat.

MAESTRO. Italian word meaning Pianist.

MAGIC. Make fun of it.

MAGNETISM. Fine topic of conversation, and one that will help you to "make" women.

MAID (THE). Used only to refer to Joan of Arc by adding "of Orleans."

MAID (HOUSE-). All unsatisfactory. Servants are a thing of the past.

MAJOR (ARMY). Only to be found in hotel dining rooms.

MAKE-UP. Ruins the skin.

MALACCA. A walking stick must be of malacca.

MALEDICTION. Always uttered by a father.

MALTHUS. "That scoundrel Malthus."[1]

---

[1] His name in France is synonymous with birth control.

MAMELUKES. Ancient people of the Orient (Egypt).

MANDOLIN. Indispensable for seducing Spanish women.

MARBLE. Every statue is of *Parian* marble.

MARSEILLE (PEOPLE OF). All great wits.

MARTYRS. All the early Christians were.

MARY QUEEN OF SCOTS. Pity her fate.

MASK. Stimulates wit (at a ball).

MATERIALISM. Utter the word with horror, stressing each syllable.

MATHEMATICS. Dry up the emotions.

MATTRESS. The harder the healthier.

MAXIM. Never new; always consoling.

MAY BUGS (OR COCKCHAFERS). Harbingers of summer. Fine subject for a monograph. Their total extinction is the dream of every *Préfet*. When referring to them in a speech to the farmers' grange, you must call them "noxious coleoptera."

MAYOR (OF A VILLAGE). Always ridiculous. Thinks he has been insulted when called Alderman.

MAZARINADES.[1] Despise them; no need to know any at first hand.

MECHANICS. Lower branch of mathematics.

MEDALS. Made only in classical antiquity.

MEDICAL STUDENTS. Sleep next to corpses. Some even eat them.

MEDICINE. When in good health, make fun of it.

MEERSCHAUM. Found in the earth; used to make pipes.

---

[1] Songs and pamphlets against Mazarin during the Fronde (1649–1653).

MELANCHOLY. Sign of a refined heart and elevated mind.

MELODRAMAS. Less immoral than dramas.

MELON. Nice topic for dinner-table conversation: is it a vegetable or a fruit? The English eat it for dessert, which is astounding.

MEMORY. Complain of your own; indeed, boast of not having any. But roar like a bull if anyone says you lack judgment.

MENDICITY. Should be prohibited and never is.

MEPHISTOPHELIAN. Applies to any bitter laugh.

MERCURY. Kills the patient with the disease.

METALLURGY. Very swank.

METAMORPHOSIS. Make fun of the times when it was believed in. Ovid was the inventor.

METAPHORS. Always too many in poems. Always too many in anybody's writing.[1]

METAPHYSICS. Laugh it to scorn: proof of your superior intellect.

METHOD. Of no use whatever.

MEXICO. "The Mexican expedition is the greatest idea of the present government" (Rouher).[2]

MIDNIGHT. The farthest boundary of honest pleasures; beyond it, whatever is done is immoral.

MILK. Dissolves oysters, lures snakes, whitens the skin. Some women of Paris take milk baths daily.

MINISTER OF STATE. The highest reach of human glory.

---

[1] Two entries: "*Images*" and "*Métaphores*."
[2] Eugène Rouher (1814–1884) was Napoleon III's most willing mouthpiece in various ministerial posts. The Mexican expedition (1863–64) was a dismal failure.

MINUTE. "Nobody has any idea how long a minute really is."

MISSIONARIES. All are eaten or crucified.

MISSIVE. Nobler than "letter."

MISTAKE. "It's worse than a crime, it's a mistake" (Talleyrand). "There is not a mistake left to commit" (Thiers). These two remarks must be uttered with an air of profundity.

MOB. Its instincts are always good. *Turba ruit* or *ruunt?*[1] "The vile multitude" (Thiers). "The sacred mob overran the doorways . . ."

MODELLING. In front of a statue, say: "The modelling is not without charm."[2]

MODESTY. Woman's great jewel.

MOLE. Blind as a mole. And yet moles have eyes.

MONARCHY. "A constitutional monarchy is the best of republics."

MONEY. Cause of all evil. *Auri sacra fames.* The god of the day— but not the same as Apollo.[3] Politicians call it emoluments; lawyers, retainer; doctors, fee; employers, wages; workmen, pay; servants, perquisites. "Money is not happiness."

MONKEY. "Offspring of a monk."[4] Follower of St. Onan.[5]

MONOPOLY (STATE). Thunder against.

---

[1] "The mob swarms": the point is whether the noun is to be taken as a singular or a plural.

[2] Fr: "*Galbe.*"

[3] Flaubert is playing on words to fuse several ideas—the sungod, who is also the god of poetry; the passion for gold (expressed in the Latin tag), the shower of gold, daylight and today—our times.

[4] Fr: "*Moineau*" (a sparrow) is a punning diminutive of "*moine*" (a monk).

[5] Fr: "*Congréganiste,*" i.e. a member of those religious orders put in charge of the education of young boys—whence the vulgar accusation of immorality that Flaubert records.

MONSTERS. No longer extant.

MOON. Induces melancholy. May be inhabited.

MOOSE. Plural "meese"—an old chestnut but always good for a laugh.[1]

MOSAIC. The secret of the art is lost.

MOSQUITO. More dangerous than any wild beast.

MOUNTEBANK. Always preceded by "cheap."

MUSCLES. The muscles of strong men are always of steel.

MUSEUM: VERSAILLES. Recalls the great days of the nation's history. A splendid idea of Louis Philippe's.
THE LOUVRE. To be avoided by young ladies.
DUPUYTREN.[2] Recommended for young men.

MUSHROOMS. Should not be bought except at the grocer's.

MUSIC. Makes one think of a great many things. Makes a people gentle: e.g. "La Marseillaise."

MUSICIAN. The characteristic of the true musician is to compose no music, to play no instrument and to despise virtuosos.

MUSSELS. Always hard to digest.

MUSTARD. Good only in Dijon. Ruins the stomach.

---

[1] Fr: "*Shakos*" (the military headdress) suggested as the plural of "*chacal*" (jackal).
[2] See note under DUPUYTREN.

# N

NAPLES. In talking to scholars, always say: Parthenopeia. "See Naples and die." (See YVETOT.)

NATURE. How beautiful is Nature! Repeat every time you are in the country.

NAVIGATOR. Always "bold."

NECKERCHIEF. It is proper to blow one's nose in it.

NECTAR. Confuse with ambrosia.

NEGRESSES. Hotter than white women. (See BLONDES and BRUNETTES.)

NEGROES. Express surprise that their saliva is white and that they can speak French.

NEIGHBORS. Try to have them do you favors without its costing you anything.

NEOLOGISMS. The ruin of the French language.

NERVOUS. Is said every time a disease baffles comprehension—it gives satisfaction to the listener.

NERVOUS AILMENT. Always put on—an act.

NEWSHOUND. Journalists: when you add "yellow," that is the depth of contempt.

NEWSPAPERS. One can't do without—but must be thundered against. Their importance in modern society, e.g. the

*Figaro.*[1] Serious sheets: *Revue des Deux Mondes, L'Economiste,* the *Journal des Débats.* You must leave them about in your drawing room, taking care to cut the pages open beforehand. Marking certain passages in blue pencil is also impressive. In the morning, read an article in one of these grave and solid journals; in the evening, in company, bring the conversation around to the subject, and shine.

NIGHTMARES. Come from the stomach.

NORMANS. Believe that they talk with a broad *a* and kid them about their nightcaps.[2]

NOSTRILS. When flaring, a sign of lasciviousness.

NOVELS. Corrupt the masses. Are less immoral in serial than in volume form.[3] Only historical novels should be allowed, because they teach history. Some novels are written with the point of a scalpel. Others revolve on the point of a needle.

NUMISMATICS. Related to the abstruse sciences; inspires deepest respect.

---

[1] See note under LOATHSOME.
[2] Fr: "*bonnets de coton,*" hence the allusion to the chief textile industry of the region.
[3] It is a fact that serial publication was more closely censored. Cf. the different versions of Hardy's novels.

# O

Oasis. An inn in the desert.

Obscenity. All scientific words derived from Greek and Latin conceal an obscenity.

Octogenarian. Applies to any elderly man.

Odalisques. All women in the Orient are odalisques. (See Bayadères.)

Odéon. Joke about its remoteness.[1]

Odor (foot). A sign of health.

Offenbach. On hearing his name, hold two fingers of the right hand close together, to preserve yourself from the evil eye: it looks very fashionable and Parisian.

Old. Always "prematurely."

Oldest inhabitants. In times of flood, thunderstorm, etc., the oldest inhabitants cannot remember ever having seen a worse one.

Olive oil. Never good. You should have a friend in Marseille who sends you a small barrel of it.

Omega. Second letter of the Greek alphabet, since everybody always says: "The alpha and omega of . . ."

Omnibus. Never a seat to be found. Were invented by Louis

---

[1] This theater is on the left bank of the Seine, whereas all the other subsidized houses are on the right.

XIV. "Let me tell you, sir, that I can remember tricycles when they had only three wheels."

OPERA (WINGS OF THE). Mohammed's heaven on earth.

OPTIMIST. Synonym for imbecile.

ORATION (FUNERAL). Any sermon of Bossuet's.

ORCHESTRA. Symbol of society: each plays his part and there is a leader.

ORCHITIS. Gentleman's disease.

ORDER (LAW AND). How many crimes are committed in thy name! (See LIBERTY.)

ORGAN MUSIC. Lifts the soul upwards to God.

ORIENTALIST. Far-flung traveller.

ORIGINAL. Make fun of everything that is original, hate it, beat it down, annihilate it if you can.

OSTRICH. Will digest a stone.

OTTER. Created to make caps and waistcoats.

OYSTERS. Nobody eats them any more: too expensive!

# P

PAGANINI. Never tuned his violin. Famous for his long fingers.

PAGEANTRY. Lends authority. Strikes the imagination of the masses. We need more of it, more of it.

PAIN, GRIEF. Always has favorable by-products. When genuine, its expression is always subdued.

PAINTING ON GLASS. The secret of the art is lost.

PALFREY. A white animal of the middle ages whose breed is extinct.

PALLADIUM. Ancient fortress.

PALM TREE. Supplies local color.

PALMYRA. An Egyptian queen? Famous ruins? Nobody knows.

PAMPHLETEERING. No longer done.

PANTHEISM. Thunder against. An absurdity.

PARADOX. Always originates "on the Boulevards, between two puffs on a cigarette."

PARALLELS (HISTORICAL). The choice is as follows: Caesar and Pompey, Horace and Virgil, Voltaire and Rousseau, Napoleon and Charlemagne, Goethe and Schiller, Bayard and MacMahon. . . .[1]

---

[1] French marshal of Irish descent who helped effect the transition from the Second Empire to the Third Republic. Popularly admired as a soldier and as a monarchist, he is here bracketed with the patriotic Bayard to suggest contemporary idolatry.

PARIS. The great whore. Heaven for women, hell for horses.

PARLOR SONGS. He who can sing parlor songs "kills" the ladies.

PARTHIAN SHOT. Wax indignant at such a shot, though it is in fact thoroughly legitimate.[1]

PARTS. "Shameful" to some, "natural" to others.

PASS (MOUNTAIN). Always mention Thermopylae. The Vosges are the Thermopylae of France. (This was often said in 1870.)

PAVILION. Abode of bliss in a garden.

PEDANTRY. Should be run down, unless it applies to trifles.

PEDERASTY. Disease that afflicts all men of a certain age.

PELICAN. Tears its breast to nourish its young. Symbol of the paterfamilias.

PERU. Country in which everything is made of gold.

PERSPIRING (FEET). Sign of health.

PHAETON. Inventor of the carriage named after him.

PHEASANT. Very swank at a dinner.

PHILIPPE-EGALITÉ. Thunder against. Another of those causes of the Revolution. He committed all the crimes of that dismal period.

PHILOSOPHY. Always snicker at it.

PHLEGMATIC. Good form. Makes you look English. Goes with "imperturbable".

PHOENIX. Fine name for a Fire Insurance Company.

---

[1] Fr: "*Coup de Jarnac,*" a back-handed duelling stroke typifying the unexpected.

PHOTOGRAPHY. Will make painting obsolete. (See DAGUERREO-TYPE.)

PHYSICAL TRAINING. Cannot be overdone. Exhausting for children.

PIANO. Indispensable in a drawing room.

PIDGIN. Always talk pidgin to make yourself understood by a foreigner, regardless of nationality. Use also for telegrams.

PIG. Its insides being "identical with those of man" should be used to teach anatomy.

PIGEON. Eat it only with peas.

PIKESTAFFS. At sight of a dark cloud, do not fail to say: "It's going to rain pikestaffs." In Switzerland every man carries a pikestaff.

PILLOW. Never use a pillow: it will make you into a hunchback.

PIMPLES. On the face or anywhere else, a sign of health and "strong blood." Do not try to get rid of them.

PIPE. Not proper except at the seaside.

PITY. Always avoid feeling it.

PLANETS. All discovered by M. Leverrier.[1]

PLANT. Always cures those parts of the body that it resembles.

PLOT. The heart of any play.

POACHERS. All ex-convicts. Commit all the crimes in the neighborhood. Must arouse in you a fenzy of fury: "No quarter, my dear sir, no quarter!"

POCK-MARKED. Pock-marked women are all lascivious.

---

[1] French astronomer (1811–1877) who inferred from his calculations the existence of an additional planet, Neptune.

POET. Pompous synonym for fool, dreamer.

POETRY. Entirely useless; out of date.

POLICE. Always in the wrong.

POLICEMAN. Bulwark of society. Don't say "the police" but "guardians of law and order" or "the constabulary."[1]

POLITICAL ECONOMY. Dismal science.

POLISH PLAIT.[2] If you cut the hair it bleeds.

PONSARD. The only poet who had good sense.[3]

POOR (THE). To care for them makes all other virtues needless.

POPILIUS. Inventor of a kind of circle.[4]

PORK-BUTCHER. Stories of patés made of human flesh. All pork-butchers have pretty wives.

PORTFOLIO. Carry one under your arm: makes you look like a member of the Cabinet.

PORT-ROYAL.[5] Very swank topic of conversation.

POST. Always apply for one.[6]

POULTICE. Always apply one while waiting for the doctor.

---

[1] Two entries: "*Gendarme*" and "*Gendarmerie*."

[2] An unhygienic condition of the scalp, once thought to be a disease, and formerly endemic in Eastern Europe.

[3] François Ponsard (1814–1867) tried to combine in dramatic poetry the virtues of the Classic and Romantic schools, producing rather frigid pieces which enjoyed great vogue and earned him the title of "Poet of common sense."

[4] Popilius Laenas was a Roman consul sent on a mission to a Syrian king who used delaying tactics. Popilius brought him to terms by drawing a circle on the ground and refusing to step outside his diagram until he got an answer.

[5] Famous abbey of Bernardine nuns founded in 1204 and situated some twenty miles from Paris. It was the site of miracles and controversies, and finally became associated with Jansenist theology, logic, grammar and the work of Pascal. In the nineteenth century, Sainte-Beuve gave it additional renown by his painstaking study of its history.

[6] Allusion to the fact that in France power and prestige go with official position.

PRACTICAL JOKES. Always play practical jokes when going on a picnic with ladies.

PRACTICE. Superior to theory.

PRADON. Never forgive him for having been Racine's rival.

PRAGMATIC SANCTION. Nobody knows what it is.

PRECINCTS. Very swank in formal speeches: "Within these precincts, gentlemen . . ."

PREOCCUPATION. Is active and fruitful in proportion to one's immobility, which in turn is caused by the depth of one's absorption.

PREPSCHOOL. Swanker than "boarding school."

PRETTY. Used for whatever is beautiful. "It's mighty pretty" is the acme of admiration.

PRIAPISM. A cult of ancient times.

PRIESTLY CALLING. "Art, medicine, etc. are so many priestly callings."

PRIESTS. Should be castrated. Sleep with their housekeepers and give them children whom they fob off as their nephews. "Never mind! There are honest ones too."

PRINCIPLES. Always "eternal." Nobody can tell their nature or number; no matter, they are sacred all the same.

PRINT. One must believe whatever is in print. To see one's name in print!—some people commit a crime for no other reason.

PRINTING. Marvellous invention. Has done more harm than good.

PROBLEM. "Need only be stated to be solved."

PROFESSOR. Always "the learned."

PROGRESS. Always "headlong" and "ill-advised."

PROPELLER. Commands the future of machinery.

PROPERTY. One of the foundations of society. More sacred than religion.

PROSE. Easier to write than verse.

PROSPECTS. Find them beautiful in nature, dark in politics.[1]

PROSTITUTE. A necessary evil. A protection for our daughters and sisters, as long as we have bachelors. Should be harried without pity. It's impossible to go out with one's wife owing to the presence of these women on the boulevards. Are always poor girls seduced by wealthy bourgeois.

PROVIDENCE. "Where should we be without it?"

PRUNES. Keep the bowels loose.

PUDDING (BLACK). A sign of revelry in the house, indispensable on Christmas eve.

PUNCH. Suitable for a stag dinner. Cause of mad gaiety. Put out the light when setting it aflame: it will make fantastic shadows.

PYRAMID. Useless edifice.

[1] Fr: *Horizons.*

75

# R

RABBIT PIE. Always made of cat.

RACINE. Naughty boy![1]

RADICALISM. All the more dangerous that it is latent. The Republic is hurtling forward into radicalism.

RAFT. Always "of the Medusa."[2]

RAILWAYS. If Napoleon had had them, he would have been invincible. Talk about them ecstatically, saying: "I, my dear sir, who am speaking to you now—this morning I was at X; I had taken the X train, I transacted my business there, and by X o'clock I was back here."

RAILWAY STATIONS. Gape with admiration; cite them as architectural wonders.

REDHEADS. See BLONDES, BRUNETTES and NEGRESSES.

REGARDS. Always the best.

RELATIVES. Always a nuisance. Keep the poor ones out of sight.

RELIGION. Part of the foundations of society. Is necessary for the common people. Yet we mustn't overdo it. "The religion of our fathers . . .": this must be uttered with unction.

REPRESENTATIVE OF THE PEOPLE. To be elected—the height of

---

[1] Allusion to Racine's love affairs in the early part of his life.
[2] Famous painting by Géricault (1819) based on a contemporary story of shipwreck.

76

glory. Thunder against the Chamber of Deputies. "Too many talkers there, they never do anything."

REPUBLICANS. "The republicans are not all scoundrels, but all scoundrels are republicans."

RESTAURANT. You should order the dishes not usually served at home. When uncertain, look at what others around you are eating.

REUNION. "A good time was had by all. Most of us will never forget it." It never breaks up without plans being laid for the one next year. The life of the party must not fail to say: "All, all are gone, the old familiar faces."

RHYME. Never in accord with Reason.

RIDING (HORSEBACK). Excellent exercise for reducing. E.g. all cavalry officers are thin. Excellent exercise for gaining weight. E.g. all cavalry officers are pot-bellied. "When he gets on a horse he's a regular centaur."

RING. Worn on the index finger, is *distingué*. Worn on the thumb, is too Oriental. Rings will make your fingers misshapen.

RONSARD. Absurd, with his Greek and Latin words.

ROUSSEAU. Believe that Jean-Jacques Rousseau and Jean-Baptiste Rousseau[1] were brothers, like the two Corneilles.

RUINS. Induce reverie; make a landscape poetic.

---

[1] Jean-Bapiste Rousseau (1671–1741) was an epigrammatist and would-be lyric poet and no connection of his namesake Jean-Jacques.

# S

SACRILEGE. It is sacrilege to cut down a tree.

SAFES. The combination is really very easy to outwit.

ST. BARTHOLOMEW. Old wives' tale.

SAINTE-BEUVE. Ate nothing but delicatessen on Good Friday.[1]

ST. HELENA. Island famous for its rock.

SALON. To write up the Salon is a good beginning in literature; it allows a man to cut a figure.

SALT CELLAR. Upsetting it brings bad luck.

SAPPHICS AND ALCAICS.[2] Sounds good in a critical article.

SATRAP. Rich man of loose morals.

SATURNALIA. Festivals of the Directoire period.[3]

SAVINGS BANKS. Only encourage servants to steal.

SCAFFOLD. When upon it, manage to say a few eloquent words before dying.

SCARF. Poetic.

SCENERY (STAGE). Isn't real painting. The only skill required is

---

[1] Though Sainte-Beuve was reconciled to the Empire and well-treated by authority, he was thought to be a malicious freethinker. A dinner given by him on 10th April 1868 (Good Friday) gave rise to rumours that "an orgy" had taken place. The guests included Flaubert, Taine, and Renan.

[2] Fr: *"Saphique et Adonique."*

[3] See note under DIRECTOIRE.

to splash paint on the cloth and smear it with a broom—distance and lighting do the rest.

SCHOOLS. Polytechnique: every mother's dream for her boy (*old-fashioned*). Panic of the bourgeois during insurrections when he hears that Polytechnique sides with the workers (*old-fashioned*). Just say: "At the School" and people will think you're a graduate. At St. Cyr: young aristocrats. At the School of Medicine: all subversives. At the School of Law: young men of good family.

SCHOOLTEACHERS (WOMEN). Are always from families in reduced circumstances. As governesses in the home, dangerous: corrupt the husband.

SCIENCE. "A little science takes your religion from you; a great deal brings you back to it.

SCUDÉRY. Snicker, without knowing whether the name is that of a man or a woman.[1]

SEA. Bottomless. Symbol of infinity. Induces deep thoughts. At the shore one should always have a good glass. While contemplating the sea, always exclaim: "Water, water everywhere."

SEALED. Always preceded by "hermetically."

SEASHELLS.[2] You must bring some back from the seashore.

SEASICKNESS. To avoid it, all you have to do is think of something else.

---

[1] It is in fact the name of a man and of his sister, both writers. Georges de Scudéry (1601–1667) was a prolific playwright in verse whom Boileau ridiculed for his bombast. Scudéry's sister Madeleine (1607–1701) was one of the *précieuses*. She produced the chief ten-volume novels of the period and was still writing verses at the age of ninety-two. Scudéry's wife is also known for her letters, which have been published, but she was not a professional writer.

[2] Fr: "*Galets*," medium-sized rounded stones found mostly on the Channel beaches.

SECRET FUNDS. Incalculable sums with which the ministers buy men. Wax indignant.

SELFISHNESS. Complain of other people's; overlook your own.

SELF-SEEKING. In the provinces, any one who gets himself talked about. "I tell you, I have no secret ambitions" signifies fond of ease or without ability.

SENECA. Wrote on a golden desk.

SERIALS (NEWSPAPER). The cause of our present demoralization. Argue about the way the plot will come out. Write to the author suggesting ideas. Vent your fury when one of the characters bears your name.

SEVILLE. Famous for its barber. "See Seville and die." (See NAPLES.)

SHEEP'S GUT. Used only to make toy balloons.[1]

SHELLS (ARTILLERY). Designed to make clocks and inkwells.

SHEPHERDS. All sorcerers. Their speciality is conversing with the Virgin Mary.

SHIPS. All the good ones are built at Bayonne.[2]

SHOEMAKER. Let the shoemaker stick to his last.[3]

SHOE POLISH. Only good when made at home.

SHOES (WOODEN). All self-made men first arrived in Paris wearing wooden shoes.

SHOTGUN. Always keep one in your country place.

SIGH. Must be exhaled near a woman.

SINGERS. Swallow a raw egg every morning to clear the voice.

---

[1] Possibly an allusion to the advent of rubber in the manufacture of contraceptives.
[2] Seaport at the southernmost end of the Bay of Biscay.
[3] Flaubert gives only the Latin: "Ne sutor ultra crepidam."

Tenors always have a "golden, bewitching voice"; baritones a "warm, well-placed voice"; basses "a powerful organ."

SINGLE STICK. More to be feared than any sword.

SITE. Place for writing verses.

SKIFF. Any small boat with a woman in it. "Come into my little skiff..."

SKIN (BLOTCHY). Sign of health. (See PIMPLES.)

SLEEP. Thickens the blood.

SNAKES. All "venomous."

SNEEZE. After saying "God bless you! start discussing the origin of this custom. "Sneezed": It is clever raillery to say: "Russian and Polish are not spoken, they are sneezed."

SOCIETY. Its enemies. What destroys it.

SOIL (THE). Grow tearful about it.

SOLICITOR. More complimentary than lawyer. No longer to be trusted.[1]

SOLID. Always followed by "as a rock."

SOMBREUIL (MLLE DE). Recall the glass of blood.[2]

SOMNAMBULIST. Walks at night on gabled roofs.

SON-IN-LAW. "My son, it's all off."[3]

---

[1] Two entries: "Tabellion" and "Notaire". Their function does not exactly correspond to that of a solicitor, but the connotations are comparable, as those of "Trustee" would not be.

[2] Allusion to a partly apocryphal tale of the Revolution. Sombreuil, the aged Governor of the Invalides, was arrested just before the September massacres but his life was saved by his daughter's pleas. According to the tale, she had to drink a glass of blood to win his reprieve.

[3] Possibly an allusion to the fact that the accepted suitor is immediately called "my son" (gendre), though the haggling over the marriage settlement may lead to breaking off the arrangement.

SOUTHERN COOKING. Always full of garlic. Thunder against.

SOUTHERNERS. All poets.

SPELLING. Believe it as absolute as mathematics. Useless if you have style.

SPINACH. Acts on your stomach like a broom. Never forget to repeat. M. Prudhomme's[1] famous remark: "I don't like it and am glad of it, because if I liked it I would eat it—and I can't stand it." (Some people will find this sensible enough and won't laugh.)

SPLEEN. Formerly, runners had it removed.[2]

SPURS. Look well on boots.

SPY. Always in high society. (See CROOK.)

SQUARING THE CIRCLE. Nobody knows what this is, but shrug your shoulders at any mention of it.

STACK (ARMS). The hardest duty of the National Guard.

STAG DINNER. Calls for oysters, white wine and racy stories.

STAGE COACH. Yearn for the stage-coach days.

STAR. Every one follows his own, like Napoleon.

STARK. Whatever is antique is stark, and whatever is stark is antique. Bear this firmly in mind when buying antiques.

STALLION. Always "fiery." A woman is not to know the

---

[1] Well-known hero of novels and plays by Henri Monnier (1805–1877). Joseph Prudhomme is a kind of French Podsnap, full of philistine feeling and absurd sentiments. (See Introduction.)

[2] "Dératé" is an established word which means "having had the spleen removed" and which implies light-heartedness, freedom from care. By extension comes the idea that such a person can run faster than others. Flaubert has another entry under this untranslatable word; "No need to be aware that the removal of the spleen has never been attempted on man."

difference between a stallion and a horse. A young girl must be told it is a larger type of horse.

STEEPLE (SIGHT OF, IN NATIVE VILLAGE). Makes the heart beat faster.

STIFF. Always followed by "and unbending."

STOCKBROKERS. All thieves.

STOCK EXCHANGE. "Barometer of public opinion."

STOICISM. Not feasible.

STOMACH. All diseases come from the stomach.

STOOLPIGEONS. All in the pay of the police.

STRENGTH. Always "Herculean." "Might makes Right" (Bismarck).

STROLLERS. All Parisians are. But nine out of ten Parisians are from the provinces. In Paris, everybody gorms, nobody works.

STRONG. "As a horse, an ox, a Turk, Hercules." "The fellow should be strong—he's all sinew."

STUDENTS. All wear red berets and tight trousers, smoke pipes in the street—and never study.

STUDS. The keeping of studs—a fine subject for Parliamentary debate.

SUFFRAGE (UNIVERSAL). Highest reach of political science.

SUICIDE. Proof of cowardice.

SUMMER. Always "unusual." (See WINTER.)

SUPPERS (OF THE REGENCY).[1] A greater flow of wit even than of champagne.

---

[1] See note under CHAMPAGNE.

SURGEONS. Hard-hearted. Refer to them as butchers.

SWALLOWS. Never call them anything but "harbingers of Spring." Since nobody knows where they come from, say "far-off strand"—poetic.

SWAN. Sings just before it dies. Can break a man's leg with its wing. The Swan of Cambrai was not a bird but a man named Fénelon. The Swan of Mantua is Virgil. The Swan of Pesaro is Rossini.

SWORD. The only notable one is that of Damocles. Yearn for the time when swords were worn: "a fellow as trusty as his blade . . . Sometimes, though, the sword was never put to use." "The French want to be governed by a sword."[1]

SYBARITES. Thunder against.

SYPHILIS. Everybody has it, more or less.

---

[1] Two entries: *"Epée"* and *"Sabre."*

# T

TALLEYRAND (PRINCE). Thunder indignantly against.

TASTE. "What is simple is always in good taste." Always say
this to a woman who apologizes for the inadequacy of her
dress.

TEETH. Are spoiled by cider, tobacco, sweets, ices, drinking
immediately after hot soup and sleeping with the mouth
open. Eyeteeth: it is harmful to pull these out owing to
their connection with the eye. "Having teeth pulled is no
fun."

TEN (COUNCIL OF). Nobody knows what it was but it was
tremendous. Its deliberations were carried on by masked
men; shudder at the thought.

TESTIMONIAL.[1] A safeguard for parents and relatives. Always
favorable.

THICKET. Always "dark and impenetrable."

THINK (TO). Painful. Things that compel us to think are
generally neglected.

THIRTEEN. Avoid being thirteen at table; it brings bad luck.
The strong-minded should not fail to crack jokes: "What

---

[1] Fr: "*Certificat.*" The French term has a wider meaning than the equivalent here
given, since it includes what we should call diplomas and licences. Contrariwise,
"certificate" would fail to suggest the recommendation of an employer, teacher,
etc.

is the difference? I'll eat enough for two!" Or again, if there are ladies, ask if any is pregnant.

THRIFT. Always preceded by "honest." Leads to great wealth. Tell the story of Laffitte picking up a pin in the courtyard of the banker Perrégaux.[1]

THUNDERBOLTS (FROM THE VATICAN). Laugh at them.

TIGHTS. Sexually exciting.

TIME (OUR). Thunder against. Lament the fact that it is not poetical. Call it a time of transition, of decadence.

TIPPING (ON NEW YEAR'S DAY). Wax indignant at the practice.

TOAD. Male of the frog. Its venom is very dangerous. Lives inside a stone.

TOBACCO. The government brand is not so good as that which is smuggled in. Snuff suits studious men. Cause of all the diseases of the brain and spinal cord.

TOLERATED (HOUSE). Not one in which tolerant opinions are held.

TOLLS. One ought to try getting by without paying. (See CUSTOMS.)

TONIC FOR THE BLOOD.[2] Is taken in secret.

TOYS. Should always be scientific.

TRADE. Argue which is nobler, Trade or Industry.

---

[1] Fr: 'Economie, toujours précédé de "ordre." ' The Laffitte (1767–1844) story is that of the poor boy who picks up a pin on his way out of an unsuccessful interview with an employer. He is called back, hired, and rises to become head of the firm.

[2] Fr: "Dépuratif." Depurative is accepted by dictionaries but not by common speech, hence the more familiar equivalent.

TRANSFER. The only verb known to Army men.

TRAVELLER. Always "dauntless."

TRAVELLING. Should be by the fastest means.

TROUBADOUR. Fine subject for ornamental clock.

# U

UKASE. Call any authoritarian decree a ukase: it annoys the government.

UNIVERSITY. The 'varsity.[1]

UNLEASH. Applies to dogs and evil passions.

USUM (AD). Latin expression which sounds well in the phrase *Ad usum delphini*.[2] Applies always to a woman named Delphine.

---

[1] Fr: "*Alma mater.*" This expression, common with us, has in French the touch of affectation suggested by the equivalent here given.

[2] "For the Dauphin's use," i.e. expurgated.

# V

VACCINE. Consort only with the vaccinated.

VELVET. On clothes, means distinction and wealth.

VERRES. Hasn't been forgiven yet.[1]

VIZIR. Trembles at the sight of a piece of string.

VOLTAIRE. Famous for his frightful grin or *rictus*. His learning superficial.

---

[1] Roman proconsul who plundered Sicily and whom Cicero attacked in six orations.

# W

WAGNER. Snicker on hearing his name and joke about the music of the future.

WALTZ. Wax indignant about. A lascivious, impure dance that should only be danced by old ladies.

WAR. Thunder against.

WATCH. Good only if made in Switzerland. In pantomimes, when a character pulls out his watch, it has to be an onion: this never fails to raise a laugh. "Does your watch keep time?" "The sun runs by it."

WATER. The water in Paris gives you colic. Salt water buoys you up. Cologne water smells good.

WATERPROOF. A very practical garment. A very harmful one because it checks perspiration.

WEALTH. Substitute for everything, including reputation.

WEATHER. Eternal topic of conversation. Universal cause of ailments. Always complain of the weather.

WHATNOT. Indispensable in the room of a charming woman.

WHITEWASH (ON CHURCH WALLS). Thunder against. This aesthetic anger is most becoming.

WINDMILL. Looks well in a landscape.

WINE. Topic for discussion among men. The best must be

Bordeaux since doctors prescribe it. The worse it tastes, the more unadulterated it is.

WINTER. Always "unusual." (See SUMMER.) Is more healthful than the other seasons.

WIT. Always preceded by "sparkling." Cheap as anything. "Good wits jump."

WITNESS. Always refuse to be a witness. You never know where you'll end up.

WOMAN. Member of the sex. One of Adam's ribs. Don't say "the little woman" but "my lady" or still preferable "my better half."

WOODS. Induce reverie. Well adapted to the composition of verse. In the autumn, when returning from a walk, say: "But see the fading many-colored woods."

WORKMAN. Always honest—unless he is rioting.

WORLD'S FAIR. Chief cause of frenzy in the nineteenth century.

WRITE. Dash things off[1]—the excuse for errors of style or spelling.

WRITTEN. "Well written": a hall-porter's encomium, applied to the newspaper serial he finds entertaining.

---

[1] The original has: "*Currente calamo.*"

# Y

YAWNING. Say: "Excuse me, it's not the company; it's the stomach."

YOUNG GENTLEMAN. Always sowing wild oats; he is expected to do so. Astonishment when he doesn't.

YOUNG LADY. Utter these words with diffidence. All young ladies are pale, frail, and always pure. Prohibit, for their good, every kind of reading, all visits to museums, theaters, and especially to the monkey house at the zoo.

YOUTH. "What a wonderful thing it is!" Always quote the Italian lines, even if you don't know what they mean; "*O Primavera! Gioventù dell'anno! O Gioventù! Primavera della vita!*"

YVETOT.[1] "See Yvetot and die." (See NAPLES and SEVILLE.)

---

[1] Small town twenty miles from Rouen where, in the fourteenth century, freemen assumed the title of "king". Béranger's song about one of these kings popularized the notion that the spot was an earthly paradise.